My Grace & Pie

By

Ben Stirrup

One

"Come on, just one more little push," said the midwife for about the six-hundredth time. *Little*, she says. Sod that, big pushes please, let's get this done! Easy for me to say.

How am I here? Interestingly I'm not entirely sure. I'm a 25 year old man, nice house, nice job, good social life etc... My name is Tom Skye. Nine months ago I think I was a bit more sociable than I should have been which has resulted in this current situation. Of course, I'm a decent guy and I've done the decent thing and stuck by Lucy (the woman currently going through it a little at the mo). Will it last? So far it's actually been ok, she's moved in, and we have decorated a nursery, yellow. We've been a bit like a normal couple, well, at least an arranged marriage sort of couple. Will love grow? I hope so but maybe doubt it too. Don't get me wrong, she's definitely putting a shift in here to impress me, not that I need impressing but my admiration is certainly growing! Fair play n'all, I wouldn't do it.

Let's go back to 9 months ago; I think she'll be a while yet. In a pub and had a few drinks, back to mine as you do. Not that I'm making out I am an absolute magnet to the opposite sex but on this occasion I seemed to be. Glass of orange & a slice of toast in the morning and thanks very much. *Probably* won't see you again but thanks for the boobs. Then seven or eight weeks later came the knock at the door. It was a weird feeling actually, wasn't sadness, annoyance or shock, nor was it giddiness, excitement or emotion, it was just weird. My mum would have been pleased, was my first thought followed by my second thought, would she? Grandchild? 'Yay.' From a one night stand? 'Noooo'. After a couple of days and plenty of chats I decided this was good. I was about to bring my son (definitely a boy) into my world, carry on the name and somebody to pass down my, a herm, endless wisdom to.

The problem however, was figuring out what to do with this woman, a vessel for carrying my heir as one of my friends horrendously put it. Did I fancy her? I guess so, she was pretty fit. Do I enjoy spending time with her? Sure. Can I spend my life with her? This woman I've known for about ten hours of my life and about seven of them naked?! Ah, just the thought of her naked made me think yeah of course I fucking can! So that was it, I'd made up my mind, Lucy, erm, thingy, will move in with me, we'll laugh, chat & have sex, in whatever order she liked. We'd shop together, go for Sunday morning walks whilst her belly gets bigger, have friends round for 'dinners' instead of just meeting here before going out. Fuck it, let's get a dog!

A couple of weeks after Lucy had broken the news to me, on my doorstep, I just realised I never invited her in. Anyway, we'd met a few times and chatted about what to do, we'd had no additional sex. Today I was going to tell her my plans about her moving in with me. For us and our unborn son and you know, maybe get some sex.

"What?! Why the hell would I want to do that?!" Not the response I'd anticipated, hmm.

"I can have a baby on my own you know, I don't need a knight in shining armour, or in this case, in shining Superdry shit." She continued, "You don't even have to be involved if you don't want, I just thought you should know about it."

Hmm.

"Why don't you just do what most dads do and just stick your head in every so often, that's probably best don't you think? Sorry that's probably a bit harsh, if you want to be involved more then that's great." She finally stopped for a bit.

"Okay," I start. "How about we just take it one day, or even one week at a time? I mean, we could date?" Date? What the fuck.

"What the fuck, date?! This isn't Dawson's Creek," she said with a wry smirk.

"I know! Joey would have bloody loved this kind gesture." My god I even remembered Katie Holmes' character name. Jesus, I wouldn't move in with me. Hang on, she made the Dawson's Creek reference. At least she was smiling now. Sex later.

"Look," she said. "You are a lovely guy and this is very noble but I can't help but think you're just doing it because you think you should, not because you want to."

Hmm. This could be an escape route. But do I want to? "No," I started, "I mean, I think this could be great, if it's not meant to be then we'll find out but let's let time tell us. Surely we owe it to your belly to give it a shot?"

She took her time, sipping her coffee whilst she thought about it. True it wasn't the most romantic proposition, nor the sexiest, but she was certainly tempted. I could tell by her silence and phone checking. "Well" she began, "I'm just not sure, I suppose it worked in the film *Knocked Up*."

Is she actually comparing the most important decision of my, our, all three of our lives to a bloody Judd Aptow movie?! I tested the water, "You're no Katherine Heigl pal".

A frown followed by a smile then, "Unfortunately, you *are* like Seth Rogan though." Bit harsh that. I wasn't. I actually looked a bit like a tall Paul Rudd. I grinned, did my best Seth Rogan laugh and we finished our plans as to what happens next. Oh yes, sex tonight.

The next couple of months actually went pretty well. Good in fact. We did all the things I expected. Long Sunday walks, pub lunches, cinema trips, movies on the sofa, nights out down the pub with friends, I actually had a designated driver, it was great! I met her family; bit weird but nice enough. They seemed pleased with the fact she was pregnant, don't know if they were pleased how or why but hey, I don't really care. I think her sister actually gave me the eye a bit, probably not, but maybe. No. Possibly.

Anyway, that's irrelevant because I'm not that kind of guy, honest. I decided I was getting the eye just to tell my mates to make me seem a bit interesting maybe, and the fact I wouldn't do anything about it.

Eventually, a couple of cracks started to show. We were eight months into the pregnancy, so that's about eight months and a few hours into our relationship, actually, of knowing each other. We were probably about six months into our relationship. But I had one niggling question at the back of my mind that I couldn't get rid of, I had to ask it but how do I? I'm sure you probably know what I'm thinking, why has it taken me all this time to ask but I actually hadn't thought about it until a friend asked me.

How do I know this baby is mine? I've been trying to ask this for about three months now. 'Hi honey, how was your day?'

'Oh mine was fine thanks, by the way, where you a bit of a whore when I met you?'

We've had the chat about numbers and experiences but her number (seven) doesn't answer many questions. She's twenty-two, she might not have had sex until she was twenty-two and had a crazy couple of months ending in me. No good, tonight I had to ask. Was this the beginning of the end? Surely it's a fair question? But should I have asked earlier?

It was over dinner, to be fair, a lovely dinner too. I made it but it was good! Lamb shank with mash and minted gravy, just the ticket on a cold November evening. I'd just poured my third glass of red, looked around my dining room, which was opened off the kitchen, wondering why I hadn't really noticed the subtle changes she had been making. Flowers, plants, pots of stones. What the fuck, stones? Candles. Candles absolutely everywhere. It would be the best house in the world if we were expecting a blitz tonight.

"Lucy"? I said with my best puppy dog eyes. "Can I ask you a question, one I probably should have asked a while ago?"

"Oh god" she said as her hand went to her mouth, then her hips pretty quickly. "I don't want to get married."

"WHAT"?! I jolted and knocked over my fresh glass of Pinot Noir. "Shit no, me neither, Jesus." I think I visibly shuddered.

"Brilliant, the idea of marrying me makes you shudder, lovely," she said.

"No, not you, just marriage in general, waste of money, neither of us are religious and, well, it'd be harder to break up." Probably not my best response if I'm honest. This hadn't started well. "Look," I continued, "I think we can both agree marriage is a non-starter so let's forget about that and tell me when was the last time you had sex with somebody before me?" Done, it was out there.

This pause was longer than it should have been. "I see," she began. "You're having doubts about this baby being yours and looking for an escape route."

"For god's sake."

"Oh, thought you weren't religious?"

"I'm not looking for a way out; I think it's a fair question, don't you? I should have asked it earlier on but it's a bit awkward isn't it?!"

The snarled lip didn't waiver as she responded. "Yep fair question, I mean we were in bed together about an hour after we met so obviously that's what I do with everyone."

Fuck. I'd walked into a hornets nest.

"No," I waited as she carried on. "There was nobody else in the close proximity to our ten minutes of madness."

Ten minutes? Cheeky bint.

"The last shagging I did was with my ex, Syd. That ended about a year ago so months before we were introduced that night by Charlotte.

"Who is Charlotte?" I asked as I really couldn't picture her.

"She's the girl that told me you were checking me out and came over and told you I was up for a bit of a dance," she said, more angrily than any joyful reminiscing.

"The one with the drawn on eyebrows?" I asked. "I thought she surprised me by coming up to me but she looked far more surprised with those bad boys drawn halfway up her forehead."

"That's a friend of mine!"

"Her eyebrows look like they have had a row with the rest of her face and were making a run for it."

"You can mock her but she's the reason we are together."

"Something else I can blame her for then." Shouldn't have said that.

"Anything else?" she said, still looking angry. "Would you like to slag of anymore of my friends? Julia hasn't had sex for 3 years. Gwen has size 10 feet. I mean Stacy has a mole on her cheek, do you want to take the piss there too?"

"That's a mole?! I thought somebody had glued a malteaser to her head!"

"Have you quite finished?"

"Mole-teaser."

"That's it, I'm off to bed, and you're pathetic. So to summarise, I'm not a slag but my friends are freaks. The door will be locked. Good night." She turned and walked off.

"Its 6.15pm," I said after her.

"Well I'm tired and bored!" she yelled. Couldn't be that tired to yell that loud. "And your lamb shank was fatty!"

That hurt.

The next couple of months were filled with little digs and arguments, as well as good times too but the wheels were starting to come off that was for sure. Perhaps it didn't seem that obvious at the time as we had the baby coming but now I look back it was obviously doomed.

What was happening to me and my nice, in control life? I may have just been plodding along, existing I suppose you could say but now, my life seemed filled with arguments, dirty looks, enhanced sighs, protruding stomachs and fucking candles.

Of course this was all part of it. I decided I needed a night out with my friends, who I wasn't seeing anywhere near enough. Don't get me wrong, Lucy saw her mates all the time so I'm not trying to be a hero, but there always seemed to be something else to do! It was Saturday night and I was off out to meet a few pals, Dom, Paul, Simon (not Paul Simon) Stuart and Bates. Normally a good night although tomorrow will be a write off. I was dressed and ready to go. Just need to find my shoes. At this point of our relationship, I'd convinced myself she'd hidden them to piss me off, when the phone rang. It was Charlotte, eyebrows probably closer to the back of her head now, letting me know Lucy had gone into labour. Oh my god. It was time.

Two

"One more little push and we'll be there honey," the midwife continued. Seven hours now. Never mind the woman squeezing the baby out, I wanted this over! I was crouched down by Lucy's head, my knees were killing me but nobody seemed interested, weird. Lucy was on her side with her leg lifted, sort of a cross between riding a bike around a vertical wall and cocking your leg for a pee, nothing like you see in the movies. I bet she'll even poo.

The journey to the hospital was fun. Lucy had taken my car and thus it had been left at Charlotte's (she was probably drawing eyebrows on the bonnet above the lights as we speak) so I had to borrow Paul's car as he'd just arrived to pick me up to go to town. He didn't say I'll drive you to the hospital but I did have to drop him at the pub. Now Paul thinks he's a bit of a boy and about 18. This car is lowered, really low, so low I was told not to go down a road with speed bumps. It has fluorescent lights and a huge speaker. He also for some reason has a tiny steering wheel with a huge fluffy grip around it. Going round a roundabout was like jacking off a poodle. Oh and the car is bright green too with a '*Shit Happens*' sticker on the back window. *I'm not bringing my baby home in this*, I thought. I made it to the hospital, and all the roads of course were literally covered with speed bumps. *What do ambulances do?* I thought. They must have a different way in. Perhaps I could find that? Nah, I left it on the road just outside the hospital and made a run for it. I don't think it was yellow lines but it deserved a ticket for being shit.

I rushed into the maternity ward, that's a lie, I rushed to the door of the maternity ward before waiting an eternity for 'Barbara' to come and vet me for entrance and finally buzz me in. Now I know nurses are the busiest people in the world but Barbara wasn't a nurse, she was a receptionist who joyfully informed me she was off looking for a new pack of biscuits. Don't worry, digestives are far more important than new life I'm sure. I suppose the counter argument would be that I'm not exactly needed now; my main input was 9 months ago. I'd disagree of course.

But, if I'd known I'd still be here 7 hours later I'd have offered to go to the shop for Barbara.

I found Lucy in the waiting room, with her mum. They filled me in on how her waters hadn't fully broken so it was going to be a while. We waited a bit, got us some tea. I could have murdered a digestive, bloody Barbara.

After an hour or so and having been told to walk around the hospital to speed things up the nurse was back and said, 'let's av' a look then love', at least I hope she was a nurse. We went off to this side room, the nurse had a big torch with her, I mean big too. Like the ones you have in your car boot because the spotty kid at Halfords convinced you that you needed it. About the size of a car battery and bright yellow. What did she need this for?

Turns out it's to have a good old look up the ol' love tunnel. Poor Lucy was sat on a bed, legs apart with a nurse and a huge torch up in her gown. The torch didn't work that well and she had to keep hitting it.

"Bloody batteries", she must have said it six times. She turned and asked me, "Have you got a torch on your phone?"

Fuck me, what? "Erm, yeah," I replied unsteadily.

"Give it here then, they're better torches on there anyway."

"Seriously?" I reached for my phone slowly and handed it over. "Don't bloody lose it in there, and don't accidently take any photos, I'll be suicidal," I said, maybe a touch self-absorbed.

I sat in silence maybe stealing a glance too often to try and see what my phone was up to. Lucy's mum tried bits of small talk but I could see she was probably the most nervous out of all three of us, don't know why but she was very jittery.

"Still not there yet dear," the nurse stated. "Go and have another stroll, help bring baby on."

Jesus Christ. Brilliant, let's go and have another slow mooch around Death Valley, can we take the route past the renal ward again please? The smell is just wonderful.

"Come on then," her mum said. "I'll treat us to a cuppa." Deep Joy. I'd rather hit the renal gang.

I reckon we were on our second loop of the hospital. We'd had our pit stop with luke warm, machine thrown-out tea and were passing the cafeteria again when something happened.

A weird noise was coming out of Lucy, top end. She said we needed to get back. Something had definitely happened!

We got back to the maternity ward. Buzzed the buzzer and yes, waited for Barbara. She finally showed up, why she was on at this time of night I don't know, keep team moral up maybe? Maybe she didn't have a kettle at home. But she showed us through back to where we'd been waiting early and told us to, well, wait. Again.

It was only about ten minutes before the nurse showed up. I had my phone and just handed it to her without any words, what words were there?

"Right luv', I think we are good to go! Are you ready for baby?" The voice from between Lucy's knees came.

"I see it's a straightforward pregnancy so we'll take you to the midwifery ward." She continued now just about standing upright and removing her gloves. I'd love to know how many pairs of gloves hospitals got through a year. Probably a couple of million quid of the NHS budget goes on them. Mind you, you couldn't exactly not have them I suppose. Anyway, why was I thinking about sodding gloves?! Slightly more important events were about to begin.

We were lead down one of the many corridors and off to the left into a room, which I'm not joking, was amazing. It was beautifully decorated, there was a spa bath, a bed with a nice fluffy duvet, a little kitchen with a kettle and biscuits (don't tell Barbara was my first thought) and a Wi-Fi speaker with some lovely soothing wave noises coming out of it. There was even a rug. Which I thought might be a bit rank but there it was, looking soft and clean.

"Make yourselves at home. Lucy get up on the bed and get as comfortable as possible and I'll go find Sarah, who will be your midwife, I don't think you've met her yet," said nurse phone stealer, never did get her name. And she left the room.

"Wow," I started. "This is pretty nice, I've stayed in worse hotels."

"It's pretty good isn't it," Lucy replied between faster breaths.

"Good? This is bloody Margate, I reckon it's probably the nicest room in the whole town!" Her mum chipped in. "I'll stick the kettle on shall I?"

Blimey, old people and their tea. She filled it with water and stuck it on as I sat down on the rather comfortable big sofa. Took my phone out, gave it a quick wipe, just in case, and asked Lucy if she was ready for me to update the world, Facebook.

Before she could answer in came the midwife, with a man in a suit.

"Hello, I'm Sarah and I'll be helping you bring baby into the world tonight," she said with a big smile, real or fake who knows or cares, whilst she flipped through Lucy's chart.

"Ah, yes thought so," she continued, more to the suited man than any one of us.

"Yes," the suited man took over. "Unfortunately you're not classed as a standard labour now as it appears your waters may have broken some time ago and there may be a risk of infection. So we are going to have to move you on to our labour ward," he said with an attempted surge of enthusiasm.

"But I like it here," Lucy mustered between struggles.

"Come on, we'll have you there in no time, its only down the corridor, best get a wriggle on incase baby wants to put an appearance in in the corridor hey," he said.

Erm. Fuck off was what I wanted to say, but settled for a diplomatic one. "Well, just in case, let's stay here," I said still actually wondering who this guy was, but he was definitely calling the shots. Probably got one of these stupid titles like *Happiness and Resource Manager.*

It fell on deaf ears and Lucy was getting scooped up and shimmied out the door, I followed with the bag. And the other bag; well she followed behind us but was looking longingly at the kettle as it clicked to its boil.

"Here we are," said Sarah the midwife. "Let's get you comfy and get this show on the road?"

Oh my god, where were we? This room looked like an Eastern European torture room. Apparatus all over the side, or tools. Stirrups were already fixed and just waiting for a couple of calves, the room was a sort of faded purple with chunks of wall missing and there was an old door with a lock on it, screams coming from the other side.

"Ah, now this is more like Margate," her mum said, holding the kettle from the other room.

Lucy looked a bit like a lost rabbit, a heavily pregnant lost rabbit, but still she wasn't sure what to do. Could we really bring a baby into the world in this room? Obviously people do as I think there were bits of placenta on the floor still. Okay, I'm exaggerating but it didn't seem far off. She settled into her bed, no fluffy cover here, just a coarse blanket, you know the type that itches you, actually, scratches you, and an off white sheet and pillow. To be fair by this point I don't think she cared where she was, she just wanted to get this person out of her!

I say it took seven hours to get even close to this baby showing their head, literally. But I don't remember all of it. After about six and a half hours of huffing, puffing, the odd yell, getting hooked up to a few machines, including, I think towards the end, one stuck to the baby's head. Yep, whilst still inside her. I was sat in one of those really uncomfortable chairs, the ones where the head of it is about a foot further out than where the base of your back needs to go, god knows who designed these but they seemed to be in every hospital everywhere. The only way I could get comfy was to tuck my leg under my other leg and a bit under my bum. I'd been told we could be in for a long night, they hadn't said this in front of Lucy, so I should try and get a little power nap but not to go far, so I didn't go anywhere but managed to close my eyes on this chair at the bottom of the bed. I moved it to the side of the bed.

I must have gone off to a deeper sleep than planned because I woke up to an almighty scream, it was Lucy and it looked like this was it. I jumped up all startled, forgetting my leg had been tucked under myself and therefore gone dead. I tried to stand on it but it gave way. Because of this, I had nothing to grab onto and fell head first into the metal frame at the foot of the bed. Brilliant.

The midwife and nurse just glanced but were obviously busy elsewhere, although I imagine they were suppressing howls of laughter and figuring out how to tell this in the staff room later. I staggered to my feet, I'd landed on my nose and mouth and blood was everywhere, oh, and my front tooth had been knocked out. Marvellous, I now looked like a beat up hillbilly. Lovely way to greet my kid. Luckily they wouldn't remember right?!

I was now back on my feet, a bit wobbly, when the nurse told me that it looked nasty. Thanks. I dragged myself up along the bed to get to Lucy's head, I'd fallen perilously close to 'the danger end'. I made it to the top end, the stirrups had been removed and she was on her side. I grabbed her hand and told her she could do this, she looked at me and screamed. I still don't know if it was in pain at one of these final 'little' pushes or the fact my face was a mess. Either way it hurt my ears, and my hand and if one of them was true, my ego.

A couple more screams and huffs and puffs and then after one almighty noise I chanced a look down towards the feet but staying near her head, and saw it. A small, very hairy head escaping. It was like a cheap sci-fi movie but one push later the rest was out and there was screaming. Little lungs screaming, the horror film torture screaming had stopped.

And that was that, I had a child, my life will be forever changed, my child was now, wait hang on, what have we got?! It's missing something!

"There we go mummy, a beautiful healthy little girl," the midwife said. "Do you want to cut the cord?" looking at me and handing me some scissors that looked broken.

"Sure," I said nervously, taking the bent snippers. I suppose there's no chance of me snipping the wrong bit as it was a girl. A girl, I was really expecting a boy. Hoping for a boy if I'm honest. I know you say 'as long as it's healthy I don't care' blah blah. Bollocks, everyone wants one or the other slightly more.

I had the scissors and the midwife put them onto the chord and pretty much put her hands either side so I couldn't actually do it anywhere other than the exact bit she was making me do it, not that I was complaining but she obviously thought I was a complete idiot. Don't know why as I stood there shaking with blood all over me and a tooth missing.

I dropped the scissors. Of course I did but never mind, I'll just grab them again. What the fuck have they landed in?! They'd landed in a grey cardboard sort of bowl, that same material the McDonald's drink holders are. I don't know what was in there but it looked like something a butcher would burn. I'm not getting them out of that.

"Can we get another pair please, Mr Cool here has dropped them," the midwife said, not smiling.

I was given another pair and it was take two. I cut the umbilical cord, weird, weird texture. I guess sort of like cutting through one of those tubes you'd connect the Bunsen burner to the gas with at school. Of course whilst I'm fannying about with all this, poor Lucy just wants to hold her baby. The baby is subsequently passed up to her, away from me as quickly as possible. I'd definitely have been a dropper the way things were going. I went and joined her up by Lucy and we held her together, well she held and I leaned in and sort of stroked her head. Then her mum asked us to look up and say cheese.

My babies first photo in this world has me in it looking like I'd just been mugged. "Thanks Iris," I chirped. "Can we do that again once I've cleaned up a bit?"

"Oh nonsense, you have to collect these moments as they happen, it'll be a funny story to tell her when she gets older."

Lucy lay there just cradling her greatest achievement, ignoring us all with blissfulness in her eyes. I knew there and then she'd be a great mum to this little cracker. She looked up and said, "I think we should call her Lola."

"Fuck off!" She's going to be a terrible mum.

"Why not? I like it," she said with a face that was part exhausted - part 'I'm having this'.

"Let's not decide now, you know I like Ethan but its turns out you grew a girl so I need time to think."

"Actually," the nurse appeared from between Lucy's legs and continued, "the male determines the sex of a child, not the mother."

"Thanks for that," I returned "Do you mind just concentrating on stitching up the one arsehole at the moment?"

Lucy to my surprise let that go, think she even giggled, which is weird considering it was her arsehole.

"From my experience the male very rarely gets to dictate the sex," Iris added before turning and leaving the room, I'd imagine to phone people and spread the word that all was ok. It turned out she'd just gone off looking for a cup of tea.

We spent the next morning, all three of us (Iris had gone) just drifting in and out of sleep and smiles. Our new little bundle of joy. Born at 3:43am on the 9th December. All 6lb 5oz of her was adjusting to her new surroundings, probably wondering if she was going to get a name before her 16th birthday. We asked for no visitors in the morning, obviously Lucy was knackered and there was still plenty to learn, like breastfeeding. Which is *the* weirdest thing ever. "But it is the most beautiful, natural thing in the world," Lucy and the nurses had said several times. I knew this, but there was a baby sucking on it.

As the day got on, Lucy had her first wee! *Take a cup of water with you*, she was advised. I thought, is that in case she's in there a while? But no, it's to pour on your twat to help the stinging. This had to be a wind up? Lucy actually said if it is to pour on her twat I'd best go in there with her so she could pour it on me.

We were told we could actually go home later that day. It sounded crazy, were we anywhere near ready? Can one of those nurses please come and stay too?! I said it to Lucy when one of the uglier nurses was in the room, not a pretty one as that would take on a pervy twist. So we started getting our stuff together, packed everything we came in with and got ready to leave with it. And of course, with a small human. Less than 24 hours after going in for her to come out, we were going out because she had. We gave a wave to Barbara, I'll send her a pack of biscuits I think, and we were on our way.

We'd let people know we weren't at hospital but they could come the next day to see us, us? Lucy and pinkie, I'd be on tea duty I'd imagine. We stopped at the petrol station to get tea bags, coffee and milk (we would need loads for the next couple of days no doubt), plasters and bandages for my 'gone ten rounds with Tyson' face and we grabbed fish and chips and we were home.

"What about Molly," I dangled.

"What, as in good golly Miss? Maybe if she was a big black woman in early twentieth century Alabama I might consider it!"

Bit harsh that. Maybe she will grow into a big black woman with an American accent. She's small and pink now but who knew?

The fish and chips were good, the name debate was not. We decided to sleep on it and we'd pick a name tomorrow. I mean it's not that important is it, only her whole life she'll be stuck with it if it's a shocker.

"We could even ask for suggestions," Lucy said before rolling over, she wouldn't sleep that much that night, scared to just in case. I was out like a light, my face throbbing and tooth missing, it was probably concussion! That's what I claimed the next morning as I was getting moaned at anyway.

It was 10am by the time the doorbell went for the first time. I was holding the baby so Lucy went. She came back in, a bit sheepishly and said, "This is Syd."

"Syd? Syd who?" I enquired as I looked up.

It was Syd Lucy's ex. Syd was a girl. Why had I never known this?

The next hour or so was what you would call a tad tense. Syd, as it turned out, is lovely. From Italy, her name was short for her surname, can't remember what, Syddietti or something stupid. God knows what her first name is to make her want to be Syd. But of course, I was itching for her to sod off so I could grill Lucy. I was fidgety and wouldn't settle. But was I angry? No. Why would I be? I'd much rather she'd spent a couple of years down necking on a lady-bit rather than a big ol' dong but even so, I thought she might have mentioned it. Especially when drunk. And *especially* when we had talks about trying different stuff out, bring a mate etc.. Not that any of that was ever serious. Maybe it should have been?!

Also, had Lucy got changed? Tidied herself up, hair done, giggling, very touchy feely. Fucking lesbian.

Syd finally left, there was definitely something there between them, or am I just paranoid? Jesus, I'd just had a daughter with this woman, I needed to chill out and relax. But what if lesbianism runs in the family, I could be sat here holding a future rug muncher? Then again, I think I'd prefer that to.. I'll stop there. With a shudder.

The next few days as you can imagine were filled with visitors, Lucy's friends only speaking to the baby in voices an octave higher than surely was necessary. My mates had been brought around by their girlfriends and wives. Maybe just to take the piss out of me because they now know about Lucy's ex, or ex's maybe? What's the ratio here? Have to save that discussion for later when neither of us were so knackered.

Still no name though. This poor girl was three days old and still being called baby or baby pink, or unicorn rainbow sparkles or whatever stupid words get put together in baby talk. Lucy had suggested some absolute whoppers, Hetty, hatty, kitty, Ginny, Toni with an I, and Tony with a Y.

"Why does it have to end in an eee?" I asked I was suggesting the other end of the scale. I liked Margot, Enid, Megan, don't know why but they just seem a better fit when she's in her thirties. Mind you, in thirty years perhaps every name will rhyme with shitty.

It was over dinner on day four of being home when something strange happened. We were eating a nice chicken and ham pie I'd made, from scratch, I do like making pie, pastry is a bit naughty midweek but who was I kidding, I'd just had a kid with a crazy clunge grabber so I may as well get fat. Anyway, Lucy was telling me about her shopping trip with the baby and she got talking to a lovely woman (hopefully not about hooking up) but when they went their separate ways she found out her name was Grace.

"So, how about that?" she asked. "You know, but Gracie"

Her and her bloody eee's.

I sat there, chewing on my, I have to say, delicious dinner and actually thought that I really liked that name. Not Gracie, but Grace. It's cute for a baby, can't have it taken the piss out of you as a teenager and pretty respectable as you get older.

"Yeah, I actually really like it, Grace though, not Gracie. Officially I mean, if you want to call her Gracie that's up to you but we can't put Gracie on the birth certificate."

"I can put what I want on it, and leave off whatever I want," She returned. I think to have a pop to say I don't have to be on it. What is her problem?!

"Well, I'm coming with you tomorrow so you don't stitch me up." I said it in a way to try and keep it like a joke. To be fair, she was smiling now, don't think it was because I'm going on the birth certificate (something I always took for certain anyway). I don't even think it was the pie making her smile. I think it was because we finally had a name for our little beauty.

THREE

Grace Millie Garside-Skye was coming up to four months now. (I had to accept the Millie as a compromise. I suppose I quite liked Molly so not too bad and she wanted her surname first, again I wasn't keen but Grace Garside-Skye sounded better than Skye-Garside I thought. Poor kid, she'll never fit her name in a box.

The first four months had flown by. I had gone back to work after two weeks paternity leave and Lucy seemed to be enjoying life, even enjoying it when I was around too. Bonus. I've got to admit, it was really nice coming home to food cooking, and in fact, back to a family. Yep things were pretty good I thought. What's the next step? I don't want to get married, I'm almost certain Lucy doesn't. But is that the logical step? I needed some advice. Time to arrange a long overdue night out with a few mates. I'll swing it with Lucy by saying she should go out Friday, Grace was a good sleeper so I could watch what I wanted whilst she was asleep, and then I'll go out Saturday. Yep, definitely that way around because I won't have a hangover when it's just me and the baby, I'd have backup.

Lucy was up for it, plans were afoot. But she went out Saturday, me Friday. Damn it.

"No way are you going to marry that axe wound-loving moody bint," said Stuart. He wasn't one to beat around the bush. "Think about it," he continued, "you don't even know her, you didn't even know that she drove on the other side of the road throughout most of her pube owning life. Sack it off and sack it off now, trust me!"

"Well it's not really that simple mate is it? She's just had our kid."

"So My Billy is six. There are thirty-two kids in his class; do you know how many still have parents that are together? Zero, not even one."

"Bollocks," Said Bates, another mate of mine that I'd known most of my life, as I had Stuart and Paul that were both here tonight. You know, cheering me up.

"How could you know that? You never see him. Never mind pick him up from school and chat with the school run mums and dads."

"Well ok, but I reckon none of them are, it's just not the norm these days. But you're wrong about not picking him up from school, great place to pick up hot mums," Stuart said with a wink.

"You're unbelievable, I thought you weren't looking for a while?"

"It doesn't hurt to line a few up ready for when I come out of retirement."

"My god, there's something wrong in your head," Paul chipped in. "What about Sally, I thought you were heartbroken and single life is for losers?"

"To be fair, I miss Sally," Stuart said bowing his head and taking a big gulp of his pint.

"Then why cheat on her like a hundred times?!"

"That was tit for tat, she cheated on me too. Most of mine were just payback."

This just about summed Stuart up. He went through all of high school going out with the hot girl from the year below, or sometimes two years below. Then it would change to the one that's now the hottest. This didn't stop when we left school, college and university he'd always have the pretty one on his arm, pretty and pretty young. He had a kid at 19, very rarely sees him as he doesn't speak to the mum anymore. We thought he'd found a bit of happiness with his last girlfriend, Sally, but that 'in love' part didn't last that long, it lasted until a new barmaid started at our local. After that, when Sally found out he was pulling more than his pints, more like his pants, she got even. Then he did with the woman at the butchers, and then she heard and bedded his bookie and so on and so on. No wonder he's a bit messed up actually, this went on for nearly two years.

"I think my friend," Paul added, "she was paying *you* back each time."

"Say what you like," Stuart said. "At least she kept me on my toes."

"She kept you in the clinic," I chirped in. "Anyway, can we talk about my problems now please. We haven't got the forty years to sort out his messy life."

"Sorry mate," said Bates, "but I think our domestically challenged friend is right. It's a non-starter. Get on your bike and peddle away. If you want the kid, E.T. her and stick her in the basket but get gone."

Well, I wasn't expecting this. I realised my friends were actually harsh heartless bastards!

"This is brilliant, thanks guys. Should I just not go home ever again then, run from here? In case you didn't realise, it's not just me or just her, its Grace. I want her in my life as much as possible."

"Until she cries you mean," Said Paul.

Now Paul, he wasn't the brightest of my friends, a bit of a Trigger from Only Fools and Horses. He wouldn't go and watch Ocean's eleven at the cinema because, and I quote – 'I haven't seen the first ten'. We told him once that Stevie Wonder had spent millions trying to find a cure for blondness. He didn't get it and brought it up at a business meeting as a fact he'd read in the paper. Yep, he was one of them, but I valued his opinion and he'd always say it as it was. But I wasn't accepting that comment.

"No, not at all. I'm sure I'm just overly emotional at the minute and I'm not thinking straight, but I want to do the most I can to be part of this little creature's life and the way I see it, making that the most likely outcome is to marry Lucy."

"Jesus Christ, you're so gay!" said Bates.

"Mega gay," added Paul. "Where's my friend gone, he's turned into fucking Bok Wan."

"It's Gok you idiot," Stuart said, "and come on guys, he's not gay. But his dirty pasty-loving bird is." We all had to have a little laugh at that. Not that I should be laughing, this was my life.

"Look," Bates started, "I think marriage is a good thing. Maybe this will be the start of many happy years as a happy family. A few more kids, happy home. Be like me, happy wife, happy life."

Bates, we all called him that because he didn't like his first name, Norman. Yep, think his parents hated him at birth. Some kind of psycho you might think. We certainly did, hence calling him Bates. His actual surname was Banks (I think). Apparently, Norman was his dad's name and *his* dad's name and *his* dad's name etc. Mind you, Bates stopped that trend and now his father rather pathetically won't talk to him anymore. Over the bloody name Norman. Now Bates was the sensible one of us, firstly because he refused to call a one-hour old Norman, but he also married his childhood sweetheart and has two kids, a nice house and a good job. They were the type whose lives were spent at various clubs for the kids all the time. (Maybe I'll retract my sensible comment.) His wife is called Yvonne, he's a Norman, and of course they found each other at fourteen. Their two kids that are seven and four are called Gail and Chip. No idea what goes on in people's heads but come on.

"You're only happy because you found somebody that acts like a fifty-five year old same as you *and* also has a fifty-five year old's name, same as you," Jibed Stuart.

"Don't forget the rescue rangers. Ch-Ch-Ch-Chip and Gayle Rescue Rangers!" sang Paul.

We were getting off track again. But it didn't matter if we got back on it. I realised one thing tonight. My friends were going to be pretty bloody useless with all of this. I got up and headed to the bar. "Four Jaeger bombs please Katie."

The next morning I wasn't feeling my best if you can believe that. The clock said 06:42. Next to me was a sleeping baby and a note on the pillow. 'Gone out, thanks for waking me. Wanker.'

Lovely. I did say I'd sleep on the sofa, was told that wasn't necessary. Little did she know how drunk I'd get when making life changing decisions! Still, can't do right for doing wrong it would seem. I'm sure she'll get me back tonight. Then I'll return the favour tomorrow morning and leave Grace next to her with no worries of leaving a young baby on a bed next to a drunk/hungover idiot. Is this how it would be now, petty little paybacks? My god, this was turning into a Stuart relationship.

As it was I had a great morning. I took Grace swimming, her first time. She loved it, as far as I could tell. I wasn't sure if she was old enough, she'd had her jabs but then decided she wasn't a puppy and I'm sure it'd be fine. Anyway, google said so.

After swimming we went for breakfast, she polished off a big English breakfast and I had some expressed baby milk. Or maybe that was the other way around. We went to the park then visited the Bates residence. One to see how he was feeling and probably laugh; he got the worst hangovers. And two, so I could get Yvonne to entertain Grace for half an hour. She's a good baby, not whinging or anything. In fact, it's a bit boring, but I needed a few minutes to talk at a normal volume and not add 'coochy coochy coo' at the end of every sentence. Who am I kidding? She slept 18 hours a day. But it would be nice to not have to check to see if she was breathing every forty-two seconds.

"Give her to me," Yvonne was reaching for her before I was even in the door.

"You sure," I said already getting her out the pram. "She's just woken up and due a feed if you want to do the honours?"

"You won't hear me moan."

"No and neither do I these days!" The shout came from Bates, lying on the sofa with a flannel on his head. Lightweight.

I thought he was complementing her at first about never moaning but the roll of the eyes she gave me made me realise it was a lack-of-sex comment.

"I've got to go to bingo and win if I want to hear a woman moan these days," he continued. Hungover, grumpy and a bit horny it seemed.

I didn't stay for long there, quick cup of tea, a little chat and I was gone. Jesus, it was 10:27. I'd got up, got dressed, fed and changed a baby, swam, eaten, visited a friend, been to the park, I thought it'd be at least 2pm. Oh well, I'll head home. Maybe Lucy would be home and ready to inflict damage on me face to face rather than just written abuse.

As I was walking through the front door my phone beeped. Lucy.

HI, DON'T WORRY ABOUT ME TODAY. IM OUT FOR LUNCH WITH MUM, ILL MAKE IT A BIG LUNCH & GO STRAIGHT TO CHARS FROM THERE. B BK LATE TONITE, XX

'Don't worry about me?' I thought. What about your daughter? Can I respond with anger, annoyance, sadness? I didn't know but thought I'd just reply with a simple 'okay'. A muted sign of annoyance I thought.

Now, I'm not going to lie and say I had the best day ever. It was good in a way that Grace was a good baby, a few nappy changes, and a few bot-bots with some great burps. It was actually like being out with Paul. It was a chilled day, but a bit boring. We did a bit of shopping, turns out babies get you lots of female attention. Not that I was looking, nor did I know how it would progress from 'oh my god she's so cute' to 'that's a lovely brand new baby you have there and I'm sure you are ready to have an affair' stage.

Maybe one day I'll have to explore that avenue. If I was being honest my day had a cloud over it because of Lucy's, well, negligence. Is that too harsh of a word? No, I wouldn't just go off at six in the morning and expect everything to be taken care of. Right, at what point do I text her?

Turns out Grace loves Soccer Saturday. We enjoyed the scores coming in, my team won. Grace liked Jeff shouting and keeping us on our toes. Obviously it's me that enjoys all that. Grace was just looking for a boob to suck on. Actually, I got where she was coming from. I would say they were totally out of bounds at the mo, but it wasn't just them. I was slowly, probably slower than everyone else, coming to terms that maybe this whole family idea was doomed.

I ordered a Chinese at 7pm and put Grace down just after reading *The Gruffalo*, which I already knew from front to back, followed by *The Quangle Wangle Qwee*, and she was in the land of nod.

Chinese was good. Watched Match of the Day and a movie, fed the baby and all of a sudden it was midnight. Still no Lucy. Nor a text. I wasn't texting her, wouldn't give her the satisfaction, plus, what I wanted to say needed to be said face to face. I thought I'd stick another film on and wait up for her just to show her my annoyance.

I woke up at about 3:30am, on the sofa, must have been tired from last night's effort. The baby monitor was on my chest, she was sound asleep. I got myself together and headed up to bed thinking it was weird I hadn't heard Lucy come back and demolish what was left of the Chinese. I brushed my teeth, and crept into the bedroom. An empty bedroom. What the fuck? I checked my phone, nothing. I was fuming. I text her asking where she was. No reply. But she's read it.

I had a sudden urge to pack her stuff up and bolt the door, which is exactly what I would have done, if it wasn't for Grace next door. Grace, the baby, in the bedroom next door to mine. I don't have a next door neighbour called Grace. She's called Maud.

I lay in bed wide awake, not able to get myself to sleep. I was so angry. If my legs and body were tired, my brain was wide awake. When my brain got tired my body woke up. Then at around 5am I suddenly had a panicking thought. What if something had happened to her? No, she'd read my text, just couldn't be arsed to reply. What if she'd gone? For good. Left me. Left Grace?! Surely not. She'd been great with her, the doting mother. I was being stupid. Wasn't I?

FOUR

Turned out, yes I was being stupid. In many ways. Lucy got back around 9am on the Sunday morning. I'd got up and got Grace ready for the day ahead. I dropped her to Yvonne because her ears weren't ready for what I was going to be saying today.

"Morning," Lucy said with a smile.

What the actual fuck.

"Morning?" I replied. "Are you kidding me? WHERE have you been?!"

She reached down and took a slice of toast off of my plate. I grabbed her wrist and took my sodding toast back.

"God, what's your problem Ike?"

"Are you mental?" was the best I could muster. "Where have you been for twenty seven hours?!"

"Oh right, yeah, sorry I'm a bit like that, thought you realised."

I couldn't believe what I was hearing. Was she for real? "Yeah sure, silly me. Please book yourself a 6 week cruise, see you next month. You.. we have a baby now in case you had forgotten."

"I know, but she's got a dad too, I know because I've seen the birth certificate. You needed to step up a bit."

This was not happening. I got up, grabbed my other bit of toast and calmly asked if she was right in the head.

"Look," she started, "I need a shower, freshen up, then we'll talk about this. Ok?"

"Erm.. No, we'll talk now. You can't just go off like that now there's a baby involved, in fact, even if there wasn't a baby I'd think it was a bit off! And no, I won't wait whilst you go and probably wash last night's cum out of yourself, do you think I'm stupid?"

"Oh don't be so dramatic, this isn't EastEnders!"

I knew this because they never say cum on EastEnders.

"I slept on a friend's sofa because we went back there after the pub closed and time just got away from me."

"This isn't ok you know, you can't do this. It just isn't right," I feebly responded.

"I know but I needed it, a good old release."

"I've got nothing against that but you need to be a bit more responsible and stick to plans. This just isn't normal."

"I did stick to my plans, I left plenty of boob-juice in the fridge for you and, ok I planned to be back around midnight but Syd said it would be easier to crash there than pay for a cab."

"Syd?" I feigned surprise but had my suspicions. "And what did she think of your 'boob-juice'? Bet she got a fucking barrel full."

"Oh here we go," she said with a raised voice, cheek of it. "Just because it was an ex's couch, you put two and two together and get five."

"Actually I'm putting two and two together and getting sixty-nine with a side order of scissor action!" Blimey that was poor.

"Is that what you think girls get up to all the time if they're gay? Such a Neanderthal," she said with an almighty annoying smirk. And she continued.

"It makes me sick to think that's what goes on in little minds like yours, can't I just enjoy a night with an old friend, my god. Didn't realise I had to run everything past you."

Now, I was still pretty sure I was in the right but started to feel like I wasn't.

"Okay, so it's alright if I stay at my ex's next weekend then?"

"I doubt you could find one that would let you," she retorted.

Good point. But still missing mine. "That's not the point and you know it. My point is, well, I've got about five. One, you can't just sod off for a whole day and night, you have a baby."

"We," she chipped in.

I ignored it. "Two, yes it's wrong to stay at an ex's. Three, it's easy enough to let me know what you're doing and let me know you're safe. Four, well fuck four and five, the first three are enough."

She went to answer but I beat her to it.

"Maybe this just isn't going to work? We are like chalk and cheese, it's destined to fail, we may as well knock it on the head before Grace knows any different." I wasn't sure I was doing what I wanted, or was I? Either way, it felt inevitable.

She looked at me like I'd asked her to tickle my balls. "Knock it on the head?" Is that what we are going to call it then? Knocking it on the fucking head? I bore your fucking child!"

"Well now you bore me." Nice. "I can't, nor want to live in a relationship like this. Let's do what's right and set up a plan for Grace. You stay here, I'll go to Pauls and we'll sort what's best."

She didn't look upset; to be fair I didn't think she would be. We'd given it a go, for the sake of the baby and it just wasn't going to work. This was far from the first problem but definitely the straw that's broke the camel's back. But it was important to get a good system in place for Grace so this had to be done on good terms. I'd offered her the house; surely that's a good start.

"Okay," she sat down. "I know, I know. You're right. You mean it about the house?"

Straight to the point. Shock.

"Yeah, you stay here, I'll cover the mortgage but you do the bills. Now what to do about Grace?"

"Well, I was going to speak to you about that anyway, my boss has asked me to come back full time from next month, and I'd like to,"

This was a bit of a bombshell. I was starting to think if she could give Grace back to the stork she would.

"It's not like I don't love her, I really do,"she continued, "but this stay at home shit just isn't me, and if I ever meet the person that created Peppa Pig I'll kill them."

"You know she's not even 15 weeks old, you don't have to watch it?"

"You know what I mean, I can't do this for the next four years, I miss work and I miss adult company."

I thought this was exceptionally shit if I was being honest, but who knows how a mind works? Especially after having a baby, I certainly wasn't going to push it. Plus this was a good opportunity for me to steal as much of Grace as possible!

"Okay," I started. "Well I don't want her going to a nursery this young so what do you suggest?"

Silence.

"How about a nanny?" she said like it hadn't been thought out. "Syd knows som…"

"Fuck that. I see what was going on last night now, operation part-time mum, full-time credit."

"NO! It just came up. I, we need to figure this out and she has a friend that Nannies."

"A friend hey, is she an extra from the L-Word like you two as well?!"

"You prick. It's not like a special club you know! She's a friend that is Australian and very heterosexual. In fact, I think she puts in round a bit."

"Oh brilliant, my daughter is going to be brought up by a bunch clit-ticklers and a nymph. I'm sure she'll end up completely normal."

More silence.

"Look," I started after a minute or so, "let me speak to my boss, see what I can sort out, maybe I could do work from home four days and just go in for one, you maybe do four in and one at home? Then alternate weekends or something? I don't know."

"It could work," she nodded, "and you're right, best do it now so Grace will only ever know us apart. Like so many others hey?"

"Well, we gave it a go sort of. You can't force what doesn't want to be forced. Square pegs and round holes comes to mind." We stood and embraced in a defeated hug. "Tell me one thing honestly though?"

"What's that?" she said not lifting her head from my chest.

"You didn't stay on the sofa last night did you?" I asked actually without a care for the answer.

She pulled away and started to walk towards the stairs before turning and saying.

"I licked her absolutely everywhere like she was a free ice cream," and off upstairs she skipped.

Shit, it wasn't square pegs I should have been worried about.

I should have been mad, but I wasn't, wasn't even upset nor surprised. It meant I had the upper hand in many future Grace-wars.

The next few weeks and months went surprisingly well. I'd moved into Pauls; a short term fix which was fine while Grace was still so small, but I'd have to sort something else out sooner rather than later. Work had been fine with me working from home, which is what I did, my actual home. Monday to Thursday I'd be back at my house for 7:00 and give Grace breakfast. Lucy was out the door by about 7:03 after a couple of pleasantries and I'd juggle work and feeds and entertaining until around 6pm when Lucy would return. Mondays and Wednesdays I'd take Grace back with me after her mum had seen her, Tuesdays and Thursdays I'd leave her there, which I hated. Friday's I'd be in the office then go pick her up after and take her, Saturday back with Lucy and then we did alternate Sundays. Simple.

Grace was growing up nicely. I was basically getting all the good bits and it really was a great sense of achievement every time Grace did something new. I fed her her first solid meal, well, not solid but not milk. It was pureed peas and I'm glad I wasn't there for that first nappy change after it (planned). I was there for her first smile and I mean proper smile, Lucy tried claiming one a while before but I'm sure it was wind. I got a proper smile then later I got the first laugh, real belly laugh. It was actually pretty great.

At eight months she was easily sitting up on her own, then last week she started this funny little bum shuffle, no sign of crawling but she'd shuffle on her bum to get to where she wanted and was very determined about it. Oh yes, this was lots of fun and enjoyment. Of course I was recording everything I could so Lucy would get to see it. I was just waiting for her to say that she wanted to swap back or switch a few things around. But it never came. She loved her job and had plans to get somewhere high in the company. When a company ends with 'corporation' it's normally a sign you can do well within the firm, and she certainly wanted that. I don't actually know what the company did or what she did; it was all a bit vague. And boring. Not that my job was James Bond. But life was good, my work was suffering a bit but I didn't really care, I was getting to see my baby develop into a young girl.

Her hair had gone from crazy curls going upwards to lose ringlets coming downwards. Probably won't be long 'til Lucy and the lezzas planned to shave it off or something.

Of course, this didn't last that long. Money. I was managing fine but no way was I going to afford rent on a place for us whilst still paying the mortgage. I couldn't just stay at Paul's with Grace in my bedroom with me; I'd had visions of a lovely pink nursery with stuffed toys and books lined up. Of course she had this at mine, which was now not mine. Grace was nearly nine months when things started to show the strain.

It was about 6:45pm on a Thursday, I was at work, I mean home, I mean my home that is not my home but is my work now and Lucy was late. I would normally just leave with Grace like on a Monday or Wednesday if she's ever caught up at work but this was a Thursday, not my night and no text or call to ask to swap. She fell through the door just after 7pm. And not alone.

"Honey I'm hommmme, sho shorry I'm late!" loudly and giggly. She was brought through and dropped on the sofa by Syd.

"I'll be taking Grace tonight then yeah? I'll cancel my evening I had planned."

She burst out laughing and mocking me about not having much of a life I guess.

"Yeah sure, you cancshel your plans, even though your life doesn't have anything worth cancshelling."

"Yep fine, good one," I said gathering stuff together and picking up Grace. "She's been bum-shuffling everywhere today, if you care? It's getting harder to work and take care of her, but we'll chat tomorrow hey, or maybe Saturday looking at the state of you."

"Sorry about this mate," Syd said playfully punching the top of my arm. I'd have told her not to do it if I didn't think she could beat the shit out of me.

She carried on, "She got a bit, well, we got a bit of good news. She's getting promoted at work and my contract has changed so I'll be back here from now on."

"Here? This actual house? I don't think that'll happen do you? But good news on the contract," I said getting ready to go. Don't know what she actually does for a living, nor do I care.

"Well that's just it mate." Mate? Fucksake. "We think you'll be ok to move back here because we are going to live at mine. Good news hey?"

Good news? This was fucking brilliant. But I wasn't going to show that. "Oh right, yeah good, I'll start getting my stuff sorted over the next few days then," I said not wanting to show I was ready to jump up in sheer delight and high five myself.

"Hold steady there cowboy." Cowboy? Seriously. "Will take a month or so, I need to give my tenants notice."

"Fine, plenty of time for us to get sorted."

My god this was good news. I'll get back in here, get rid of four hundred and seventy candles and bowls of pot pourri and it'll soon feel like home again. Yes, in one swift five minute period my life seemed like it was ready to fall into place.

As the next month went by, I was sorting the house anyway and they were slowly boxing up their stuff. There were a few arguments about whose stuff was whose. Obviously just about everything was mine but I let her take things like the Gordon Ramsey masher she seemed so keen on, probably for some sort of sex game, but I got one from tesco for two quid. I'd decided life was too short! I'd have to buy a few new bits for Grace, duplicates of some as I thought she'd pretty much want to take most things of hers, I was right, but I didn't mind as I actually enjoyed getting stuff again, this time with Grace so she could (sort of) pick what she wanted.

It was actually in Tesco when my happiest moment so far happened. Grace, not quite eleven months looked at me and said, "Dadda." If I'm honest it seemed a bit more like, 'Gadda' but I'll let her off. Sheer delight ran through my bones and not because she said it before mumma, but just for the warm love that oozed through your body for something so delicate and delightful. And in Grace's case, intelligence of course. Now the weird thing was I'd noticed Louis Armstrong was playing through the speakers. *All the time in the World* was the song, a good song and I was singing, very quietly, along to it, to Grace really. I say this is weird because I remember this being the song on the radio in the car when we brought her home from the hospital. I decided in the car there and then I'd make this song our song and I did sing it to her when she was going to sleep the nights I had her. But I think this was the first time we'd heard it properly. Oh yes, I had a genius in my trolley. Either that or she thinks Louis Armstrong is her dad. With the mother she had, I wouldn't have 100% ruled it out.

I obviously couldn't wait to tell the news to Lucy, and her, I don't know what, girlfriend? Lesbian life partner? I'll just call her Syd. I knew they were at mine finishing off packing up. They didn't seem overly impressed; maybe Syd was a bit annoyed Grace hadn't called her dadda first but hey. Again the strange thing was that Lucy didn't seem too bothered. If it was me, I'd demand to have her for the next three weeks and lock her in a room with me and a tape recording just playing that word over and over until she said it. Don't get me wrong, Lucy wasn't a bad mum, she was great when she was with her and maybe moments like this didn't bother her because she thought there'll be plenty of other 'firsts'. I was different, I wanted to witness every first possible, throughout her life. Hang on, maybe not every first, that gets a bit weird when she starts hitting late teens but you get what I mean. No, Lucy was a good mum with her but I worried that she didn't seem too good of a mum when she wasn't with her. Again, maybe that's how she deals with not seeing her, maybe it's normal to make the most of your 'free' time and I'm the strange one for wondering what Grace was doing those evenings she wasn't with me, cooking my dinner, for one.

It was Grace's birthday just around the corner. I thought maybe it was time to get myself back out there. Surely the younger Grace is, the easier it is to pull?! Mind you I wasn't going to compromise when it came to finding a new bird, woman I suppose I should say. Grace was, and always will be my number one lady. And what was the rush anyway? As Louis said, we have all the time in the world.

FIVE

Two weeks after that, she was walking. I was on the phone to work and Grace had pulled herself up to the edge of the coffee table, as she did quite a lot, and was shouting at me. She got my attention and motioned to start walking towards me, this had been going on quite a while now, and she'd normally drop to her bum then scoot over like some weird lazy creature. Not this time, her hand came away from the table and her first wobbly step was taken and she was heading my way. I hung up the phone, rather unprofessionally I admit. I didn't have time to grab my mobile to film it, nor get Louis Armstrong on just to tell people there's a weird link, but I just crouched down on my knees and put my arms out, making noises that you kind of say to dogs I think, but the wobbly walk was well underway. Two steps, three.. FOUR and she was nearly in my arms. The last couple of steps were massively hurried but she'd done it! A few false starts over the last few weeks but now there was no stopping her. We had a walker! Best let her mum know, but not just yet. I got her doing it again.

It was the day before Grace's first birthday. I was throwing her a party here at home. I spent all of the day and most of yesterday cooking and baking. Now I love cooking. And my speciality was pies. So this was a pie party. Obviously there's cakes and party bags, balloons and games for the kids, but there were only about five kids coming, Iris who had Grace on an afternoon each week to take her to a play group, decided to tell me yesterday she'd forgotten to hand out the invites so no other babies were coming from there, but could I save some cake and goody bags for her to take them in to them next week. Cheeky cow. But okay.

One of Syd's friends was coming with her son who was about the same age as Grace and also Yvonne's sister's kid was coming with Bates and his two (apparently she was about to turn one too so at least there's a bit of relief from Grace looking like a right billy no mates). Obviously these birthdays are about adults having a get together too and a few bottles of wine, beer, fuck it, vodka too probably.

So it was a good opportunity for me to show off my pastry making skills and treat everyone to a few pies. I like experimenting with them too, so maybe I was using them as guinea pigs but I didn't think they'd care. Of course the secret was in my pastry, which will remain a secret to my dying day, when I pass it onto Grace obviously. Today I'd made a minted lamb pie, for me as much as anyone as it was my favourite. I'd made a Philly cheesesteak pie as that was Grace's favourite (she had mainly healthy food by the way, I wasn't raising a whopper). But I'd made a few for today, never really made huge ones, just five or six medium sized flavoursome beauties, even if I did say so myself. And there was a bit of variety for people to try too. I'd made a chicken tikka bhuna pie, a Moroccan spiced turkey pie, a steak and ale pie, a chicken, ham and leek pie and finally a lentil and spinach pie, well, because there were lesbians coming. I'd done a lot of creamy mash to go with them, plus roast potatoes and boiled potatoes to try and keep everyone happy. Pie was a good dish to serve at these sorts of things because you can just put them out and people can help themselves, eat as much of one as they like or even hide the fact if they don't like one. And then of course there was jelly and ice cream. Maybe the kids would get a bit of that if they were quick enough.

The day went really well, Grace got spoilt rotten as you'd expect, I won't bore you with presents, but there were plenty of dolls and lots of pink. She did get a toy shop though off Iris, I'll try and keep that here so I can play with it. Grace was showing off walking round with one of her new dolls and being extremely cute. I relaxed a bit, she was staying with me tonight but there were plenty here to keep her entertained. So I did the circuit asking for feedback on my pies, I'm a bit sad like that. Everyone said they were delicious, Syd even said I should open a pie shop. A rare compliment, especially as I assumed she was a vegetarian and only tried one of them (I was wrong, she did eat meat surprisingly).

I walked over to my friends that were sat in the front room with Soccer Saturday on, I was surprised Grace wasn't in here; Peppa Pig couldn't hold a torch to Jeff Stelling in her eyes, honestly.

"Yeah, she just won't leave me alone, we're at it like sex starved teenagers," Stuart was obviously talking about his latest conquest and I'd joined half way through.

"I get that," Bates said, "but isn't this the dream, what you've always wanted, sex on tap?"

"Look, some people's dream is to sing Nessun Dorma at the Royal Albert Hall. It doesn't mean they want to sing it every bloody night. I can't keep up!"

Paul laughed loudest and said, "You're getting too old, can't keep up with her!"

"She is only nineteen to be fair," Stuart said, dropping that on us for the first time.

"She'll have you binned off before Christmas unless you up your game grandad," Paul continued.

"Ah what do you know you sad bastard. I tell you what, why don't you come and watch sometime? Closest you'll ever get to a hot piece of ass!"

"Oh blow me James Hewitt," Snarled Paul, with a somewhat strange reference. He soon realised this and felt the need to add, "Because he's a cad, right?"

"One," CK started, "cad? Who even says that? And Two, James Hewitt as in the bloke that had a fling with Princess Di in like, the 90s?"

CK was another friend of ours, we'd only known him three or four years but he worked with Bates and he seemed a nice bloke and he started coming out with us and so on. Of course his name isn't CK, it's Terry. We call him CK because it's short for Chinese Kojak. No, he's not bald, nor even remotely Chinese. But his parents are Greek and their surname is Savalas, so he's actually called Terry Savalas. Some people we try and explain it to aren't old enough for Kojak, neither are we to be fair, but we know who and what he was. Suppose the people that come up with nicknames linked to forgotten 70's TV shows are also the same people that reference James Hewitt the cad when trying to call somebody a male slut.

Arsenal scored and had that tool Charlie Nicholas jumping around on the screen, and a couple at the party too. I'd never actually wanted them to score before but at least it got the subject away from Stuart and the teenage sex monster.

"I'm going to sort the cake in a minute, so we'll all gather round in the back," I commanded.

"She said that to me last night wink wink," Stuart said nudging Bates with his elbow.

"Doesn't even make sense," Bates mumbled and walked away from him.

There was some sort of murmurings of acceptance to my order then CK, who was going out with an American decided to tell us a story. I thought I'd stay and listen before getting Grace and the cake; they were normally either dirty, funny or occasionally interesting.

"Well, the other night CeCe said to me," CK started and was looking over his shoulder to make sure his girlfriend wasn't listening I assume, or maybe just any woman as this room just had men in it, about ten of us. He carries on with an attempted impression of her, although I didn't know what part of America she was from. I was sure to shit not going to figure it out from this impression.

"'I just don't think you're showing me enough passion lately, no emotion, is everything okay?' So, bearing in mind we've just had sex, I was thinking this was a strange thing to say, it immediately made me think she had a problem with something, but I wasn't going to fall into that trap so I said to her, 'I'm really sorry baby, I know what you mean but not sure why' blah blah. 'How about you try a little harder for me, it'd make me feel much better about myself and us.' So by this point, I'm thinking, where is this going so I just say, 'I'll try honey but I can't just turn it on like a tap,' to which she says, 'force it'. To which I reply, 'Sorry yeah, I can't just turn it on like a faucet,' totally true. She laughed and the crisis was resolved."

"Well not really, she obviously thinks you're about as deep as one of those puddles Peppa Pig is always jumping in," said Bates.

"Oh well, we'll worry about that another day hey?" was his simple reply to that.

I commented by saying, "I wish those puddles were deeper, get rid of that sodding pig."

The rest of Grace's first birthday was good. We cut the cake, yep a Peppa Pig cake. She attempted to blow out the candle, but pretty much just spat everywhere and the rest of the time she was wobbling around on her unsteady legs with the odd tumble here and there but she was doing well. She was getting tired though and I thought it was time for us to get our birthday dance in. I decided I was going to dance with her on every birthday. Obviously to *All the time in the World*. I'd decided it'd be a nice little tradition and was interested to see what age I could get her doing it until, I was thinking thirteen or fourteen, whatever the age is they start hating you! It wasn't something I really wanted to do in front of people but it maybe seemed a bit creepy to do it on our own somewhere so I just made it look like the song came on randomly, quite randomly as it followed *Old MacDonald Had a Farm* and *Baby Shark*, but it started so I grabbed her up and danced with her. She held on tightly around my neck as I moved around singing quietly along. It truly felt like the best moment of my life so far. Halfway through the song I put her down and we finished with her dancing (sort of) and me holding her up. Nonetheless, it was still great.

It got to around seven-thirty and Grace was done for the day and was easily asleep within minutes, we only got halfway through *Huggle Buggle Bear,* that's how tired she was, but she'd had a good day and that made my day. Plus my pies went down a treat. It was a Saturday but no way was I getting a babysitter on her birthday. I'd arranged with Lucy that it made sense for Grace to stay here and I'd just let the party go on through the evening and Lucy (and Syd obviously) were welcome to stay on along with my mates. I mean, what could possibly go wrong, all drinking together and all with plenty to say I'm sure.

I set up the baby monitor, Grace was a good sleeper, but just in case she had a restless night with a bit of noise downstairs I thought I'd pretty much keep it on me most of the time or at least in eye-line of me or a sensible adult, if there was one here. I wandered downstairs and Syd was in the front room sat around the coffee table with Paul, Bates and CK. The kitchen diner had Lucy with a few of her mates, a few stragglers and Stuart. What was getting said in there I didn't want to know so I opted for the front room. All parents with kids had gone except Bates' two, they would sleep here until Bates and Yvonne, or Yvonne, wanted to go home.

I walked in the room and they were talking about CK's brother who was in the army.

"So yeah," CK was saying, "he did tours in Iraq and Afghanistan, saw some real shit let me tell you."

Paul and Bates were just listening and Syd seemed pretty interested.

"Well, we owe him a great deal of gratitude, I certainly wouldn't fight for this country, state of the people who run it, or try to."

There was a nod of approval from everyone around the coffee table.

Syd continued, "Yep, bloody mess. Can I ask you why he left the army? Sounds like he was in it for quite a while."

CK took a swig of his beer, he always claimed he hated talking about it but he always brought it up. "Well the trouble was he came back from Afghan with an amputated leg."

"That's gross," Paul said, I don't think he knew this about CK's brother. "Why didn't he leave it there?" There was a stunned silence as everyone knew he wasn't even joking.

"Erm," CK started, "I think he did mate."

I got up and left the room, conversations for morons was not on my agenda. Syd got up and walked out behind me. As much as I shouldn't like her, she was a really nice woman. And she was sensible and hard-working and idolised Grace, sometimes it seemed more so than Lucy.

"How's it going daddy?" she asked me as we walked down the hall to the kitchen.

"All good, daddy," I joked even though she is definitely the fella out of her and Lucy.

"I was thinking about that actually as it goes." She obviously had something to discuss with me.

"What's that then?"

"About what we should get Grace to call me?"

"That's a tough one isn't it, I mean Syd is really hard to say isn't it? Real tough one that, tell you what, I'll get her watching Ice Age soon and that sloth thing is in it so she can practice." Yeah I liked her but she didn't need to know it.

"Come on dude." Dude. "I'm serious, me and Lucy are serious. I'm going to be in her life now all the time and I don't want to just be Syd to her."

I really didn't understand, what was I supposed to suggest? As long as it actually wasn't dad or daddy I didn't really care either.

"Obviously you must have an idea? Why does it matter to me? I mean, personally I think Syd."

"Don't be a prick. Look, I haven't told anyone this yet and not sure why I'm telling you first, because of Grace I suppose, but I'm going to ask Lucy to marry me."

For Godsake. Really. I shouldn't have been surprised really. To be fair though, they suited each other and it made sense. At least until Lucy decided she wanted cock again no doubt.

"Congratulations," I said. "It's a good idea, nothing to do with me though, but if it's my approval or something you want, then you have it. I hardly know her in a weird sort of way."

"Thanks. Yeah it wasn't approval I was after, just thought I should run it by you."

Fair point, clever too. Shows she will do what she wants but easier to keep me sweet I suppose. Plus I didn't think it'd make any difference to me or Grace. That would prove to be a mistake.

"Yeah fine, whatever. Good Luck!" I said and turned to walk back to the front room as I didn't really want to see her go in there and inevitably snog the face off Lucy, or did I?! No, I couldn't be dealing with happy lesbians at the moment. Mind you, seeing Stuart's face when they did it would be a picture. A mixture of disgust and arousal I think. He was quite old fashioned but also a full on perv. I liked making jokes about it but I understood the modern world a lot better than him. And these other two idiots in the front room.

CK and Paul were sat either side of the coffee table. As I was walking back up the hall I could hear the conversation.

"No." It was CK. "It's so not called that, it's called the runway."

"The runway?" Paul was talking quite loudly. "What the fuck is a runway, it's simply called the tickle spot, fucking runway."

"The tickle spot, what are you, seven? Google it."

"Im not putting that in my search history!"

I walked in.

"Ere, ask Tom, he'll know I reckon." They both looked at me before Paul started talking.

"Settle this argument for us. What's the name of the thing that's between a ballbag and an arsehole?"

I looked at them both and said, "The coffee table," turned and walked out the room again.

SIX

The next year went ridiculously quickly. It only seemed to be a blink of an eye and we were planning her second birthday. She was obviously walking lots now, which slowed my day down huge amounts! Not that I minded, she was still lots of fun and really growing her character. She made me laugh every single day and I made her laugh. I made her cry, obviously she was cute as anything but if she didn't get her way, wow. I wasn't as tough on her as I should have been I suppose, but it's quite tough when you're not with the mum and you don't want to be the bad guy. Grace was too young to actually understand or use this but I was just trying to make excuses for myself really. I wasn't a push over but she did get her own way a lot. God help me when she's old enough to actually use this against me!

It was a week before her birthday and yep, it was Lucy and Syd's wedding day. Why they planned it a week before Grace's birthday I have no idea, thunder stealers if you ask me. Grace was talking really well now, she couldn't say her S's which was pretty funny, especially if she picked up a stick; it became 'dick'. Childishly this made me laugh a lot and I'd get her saying things like, 'Mummy likes stick,' which always brought a few raised eyebrows but had me rolling around on the floor half the time. I was going to get her to say it mid ceremony today but I wasn't that cruel.

Grace was a flower girl and looked gorgeous. Blonde ringlets fell down her head and she was dressed in a beautiful rose coloured outfit which she wanted to wear every day since she was shown it the month before. I promised her she could sleep in it that night if she wanted.

The wedding was quite a small event at the local registry office and went well. I was only there on Grace duty and the rest of the hall was filled with family members of theirs and a few friends, all of whom had short hair and dressed in suits, but hey, I'm not judging. There I was, sat there surrounded by women, none of whom I'd ever be brave enough to hit on! It felt like a bit of a waste. I was like superman here but couldn't fly. Jesus, what was I saying, they all looked like extras from Mad Men. I was starting to realise I needed a woman. I'd spent the last year planning an ex's lesbian wedding with the help of a one year old and apart from three different nights with the same woman to 'empty the boys', I was in need of more and it was dawning on me. Nothing would affect Grace, I'd make sure of it, but I needed to get back out there. Gemma, the girl that had stayed a few times for a bit of fun, was quite simply that. There wasn't much conversation, in fact, I think she might even have a boyfriend now so that was a non-starter. It was Grace's birthday next week and I'd invited a few from her play group again (I'd made sure the invites went home in the kids bags this time). Who knew, maybe a yummy mummy with a kid a similar age to Grace would turn up?!

Anyway, Grace was getting sent down the aisle, is it an aisle in a registry office? *Anyway, don't concentrate on that, look at your daughter.* She was perfect. Walking down there with a huge smile on her face, carrying a bunch of, I'm sure beautiful lilies but they were nowhere near pretty enough to distract from Grace. She was fantastic and she was loving it. She even stopped to spin to show us her dress, she was destined for showbiz this one, that wasn't rehearsed! She looked my way and blew me a kiss. Oh no, I think I was going to cry. SHIT.

And to make matters worse, I was going to have to get a copy of this wedding so I could keep this moment forever. *I Love you Baby* by Andy Williams was playing and nothing could have summed up how I was feeling more. It was picked for them to walk down the aisle to but Grace had stolen the show. That's my girl!

Lucy and Syd both walked down the aisle together, just in case you were wondering. Lucy didn't know her dad but Syd's dad, who looked old school military, made no secret he was sick to his stomach with this. The story I heard was it'd be a cold day in hell that he ever witnessed a daughter of his get hitched at a dyke wedding. I realised that although it was new to me and I made jokes and called them names, it was always in jest, and well, they just kept coming to me. But there was a real hard hatred in many people still when it came to it. I didn't know if I was looking forward to his speech or not. I had a feeling it'd certainly be interesting but hopefully wouldn't ruin the day.

As it turned out Syd's dad passed out before his speech, I couldn't tell if she was upset or relieved. Either way the rest of the day went pretty smoothly. I stayed until Grace could barely keep her eyes open and waited for the nod from Lucy to get her ready to go upstairs. We were in a hotel for the reception and I booked in upstairs for me and Grace. Turned out it was the room next to the bride and erm, bride. I was glad to be getting up there early, watch a movie and pass out before I could hear them going at it. Grace had had a great day, she fell asleep with a big smile, before that changed to a snore. I fell asleep mid film and we were awake for 7am next morning both feeling fresh as a daisy. We went down for breakfast but there wasn't anyone else from the wedding party. Not that I was surprised, I think it'd have gone long into the night. I text Lucy to see if she wanted us to hang around or if she just wanted to come round later. I didn't get a reply. I took Grace to the hotel pool whilst I waited and returned to a text saying that they'd see us at 4pm at mine. And off we went.

At 4pm they turned up and told me they were going on a honeymoon last minute, a present from Iris apparently and Grace was to go with them. Grace on a plane, my stomach churned, mind you, she'd love it I'm sure. And it was only the Canaries for a bit of winter sun. But five days without her? I hadn't gone two days without seeing her. Later that day, my mates convinced me it'd do me good and planned a couple of nights out. I had convinced Lucy to let me keep Grace on the Sunday evening even though they were leaving at 5am Monday but I said I'd get up and bring her to the airport myself to say goodbye.

What a stupid idea that was, getting up at 4 was ridiculous. Even more ridiculous was trying to get a sleeping nearly two year old ready, it was like moving a sleeping cat around. But we got it done and I got to the airport on time. I said goodbye to Grace, she didn't really get what was going on except that she was going on a plane. She gave me a big kiss and a cuddle and she was ready to go with her Gruffalo Trunki. I told Lucy and Syd that no matter how nice it is they'd better get her back for her party on Saturday. I wanted my dance!

They went through the check in and that was that, five long days without my baby. I didn't want to dash off and went to the viewing lounge and tried to figure out what plane was theirs so I could watch it take off. I realised I had nearly three hours to wait so I just picked the first plane I saw move and imagined that was theirs and waved it off! A cheat I know, but what was the difference really?!

I thought about what to do next; I could actually go to the office, it was early but you can get in from 5am apparently. I was closer to the office than home here but fuck it, couldn't be arsed with that. I thought I'd go back to bed but didn't think I'd be able to get to sleep. I decided to grab a Starbucks and make a decision after caffeine. I was stood in the queue, why was there always a queue at these places? It was fucking 5am. They even have you queuing twice and you're fine with it. Queue to order your coffee then queue to get the bastard. Oh and it was £4.60 for a sodding coffee.

I walked, after ordering and paying to the second queuing point at the end of the counter, and waited for my name to be called out like some sort of raffle winner. I'd given the name Adolf just for personal humour, I liked doing it, Dick, Hitler, Osama, Angus, Wolfgang. I think I'd even said my name was Pinocchio once. I was waiting at the end still shaking my head at my abysmal 40p change from a fiver when I looked up and locked eyes with a rather pretty lady. She was sat at a table nearby with her expensive drink.

As it happened, probably for the first time in my life, she came over to me. "Hi," She said, nice opening. I was expecting her to reach past me and grab a sugar or something.

"Hi to you," I sort of fumbled through a response. To be fair, it was very early.

"I saw you by the departure viewing area, saying goodbye to a girlfriend?"

Smooth. Get a bit of info early. Could this actually be the dream. Chatted up in a Starbucks by a beauty? It's the reason people put up with the pricing and queuing isn't it? Oh and the trendy Christmas cups.

"No, I don't have one." Straight to the point. "It was actually my daughter I was waving off, she's off to Gran Canaria with her mum... and her wife."

"Oh right, I won't delve any deeper into that one then." She smiled and put her hair back behind her ear. I'm sure I'd read somewhere that was a sign of flirting. Or was it just nerves. Her hair was rather nice, dark brown and smooth as silk, dark brown eyes and a lovely smile. I'd say about 5 foot 6 inches so fairly tall. Her figure was slightly hidden by her coat but my gut (and her legs sticking out the bottom) told me it was nice. I thought how can someone look this good in the morning? I'm sure I looked like shite.

"No honestly, it's fine, they were actually off on their honeymoon," try and play for a bit of sympathy.

"I see, and you're finding it hard to see your daughter off? First time I assume?"

"Yep, she only turns two later this week and I spend a lot of time with her, so this has actually been harder than I thought."

"Well, if it helps, it *doesn't* get any easier."

"That's great news, I perhaps will just ground her for twenty years." Jesus that was shit, I tried to save myself and line up a potential *asking out* opening. "Anyway my friends have told me to make the most of a COMPLETELY free week. What brings you to the airport at this hour?"

"I just like hanging around Starbucks looking for vulnerable men to hit on, I have a room over at the Hilton and take them back there whenever I can."

I was in a stunned silence. I was scrambling for a response when she burst out laughing.

"Your face! My god I think you actually believed me then?! I swear to God I've never even approached anyone at an airport, especially a man but I saw you earlier and thought I'd find out a little bit more about you. You looked oddly upset yet smiley at the same time."

"Thanks for that then, I was trying to find my inner James Bond to respond to you, I'd more likely be like Phil Dunphy from Modern Family though."

"I love that show."

"Well, me too. Maybe we can watch it together, scrap that, that's so lame! But maybe I could get your number and we could grab a coffee or something?" Such a Romeo. Or James Hewitt.

"Sure, it's not what I expected to be doing at 5:15am at an airport but why the hell not!" She started to write her number down on a napkin.

"What are you doing here at this time anyway?"

"Same as you actually, dropping my 7 year-old off. He's off with his dad for a week, and it gives me chance to get on with work."

"And meet me," I added with a grin.

"And meet you", she half smiled, "but work has been hectic and running around after him isn't easy."

"I know that feeling. What do you do?"

"I work at the university, teach history. Part time normally but it's frantic so I'm having to do a bit more at the mo. But I enjoy teaching people and especially about World War Two, how great the Allied victory was etc.. All fascinates me, even now."

"Oh yeah, I love history too. We'll definitely have plenty to talk about then!" I actually did love history.

"Great," she handed me her napkin it had her number and a little kiss and her name, I hadn't asked her bloody name.

"Thanks Kate," I was about to say my name when the Starbucks bloke shouted, "Grande Americano for Adolf!"

SEVEN

It was the day of Grace's second birthday, this time at the local play centre and more kids, made sense I suppose. Grace was back from holiday and told me she had a good time and went on a donkey. And can we get one. A pink one. Lucy and Syd looked fresh and relaxed and told me I just *have* to go there and then proceeded to tell me how everything was *the* best. You know, the barman always put extra alcohol in *their* drinks, or the cleaning lady always left *their* towels in heart shapes and all that rubbish. Yeah, just you guys I'm sure.

I'd only met Grace at the centre that morning as they got home late last night but she had facetimed me a few times so I was all in the know. When she turned up she was as excited as I'd hoped and expected. A Gruffalo cake had been ordered (she'd checked with me several times). And all the balloons were pink, another demand of hers. Now, I'd invited Kate. How to approach this one. I knew Grace wouldn't actually understand anything but Lucy might ask who the hell is this at my daughter's birthday. I hadn't said anything yet but would pull her aside for a chat.

The Kate situation. Situation is a bit of a weird word for it but it was a situation with good development potential. She, luckily, laughed at the coffee name, which was good. I was going to ignore the bloke but he looked straight at me, plus I didn't want to waste a fiver! I'd texted her later that evening, being out the loop for so long I wasn't sure if this was too keen or not and I certainly wasn't asking any of my buffoonish friends. It turned out she was glad I'd texted, nobody phoned these days did they? And we arranged to meet up Monday evening. We'd shared a bottle of red wine in a cosy little pub not far from her house apparently (not that I'd google-mapped her house of course). She only lived twenty-five minutes from me which was good, another thing I'd overlooked at the airport. Didn't ask her name or the fact people travel to the airport from all over the country.

The wine was good and the company even better. We talked a lot with not really any awkward silences. It got a bit awkward as we were saying goodbye, do I shake her hand? Ask her back? Surely somewhere in the middle. I turned out to be a smooth mother fucker and started with a kiss on the cheek before turning it into a hug so when I pulled away from the hug she kissed me on the lips. No tongue or anything, just a nice soft lip dance. Perfect. We agreed to meet again Wednesday, probably making the most of our kids being away. She was off Wednesday afternoon and I said I could easily skive off work so we met in town for a coffee around 2pm. Tough one to know what to wear, shit, I didn't really think about that honestly.

Again everything was great, coffee with lots of chat. She was filling me in on her ex. She was thirty so a couple of years older than me, which was fine. She looked at least two years younger than me. She was married to her ex, and divorced. Wow, a divorcee, I was such a grown up. She'd been with him since she was nineteen, had Connor, her son, at twenty-three, then found out her husband was cheating last year. And it wasn't his first time. I was only the second date she'd been on since and the first since her divorce ink had dried. I'd told her my story. She looked at me whilst I was telling it and seemed to be really listening. I suppose it was quite an interesting start to fatherhood, one night fling with a stark raving lesbian.

After coffee she suggested the cinema, which we did before getting dinner at a nice restaurant near the cinema. I really wanted the spaghetti but no way was I attempting to eat that in front of her, and I had a white top on (I'd decided on a white top and casual jeans, in case you were wondering). That also ruled out the burger. Trying to get my gob round one in front of her would make her run for the hills. Nope, played it nice and safe and had penne pasta, my god it was garlicky though!

Again at the end there was no awkwardness, I'd been tempted to ask her back but didn't. This time there was a proper kiss when I dropped her home, nice house too it looked like. We again agreed to meet Friday evening when I'd go to hers for dinner.

I won't go into detail but Friday evening went *very* well. Very well as in she also made me breakfast Saturday morning. I'd already decided that she needed to be a keeper. It was the Friday night I'd asked her to Grace's party. She was weary but agreed with a bit of reassurance. And we agreed I wouldn't meet Connor just yet, seven year olds are more switched on than two year olds! Plus she told me his dad could do no wrong and when he was back on Sunday after a week with him it certainly wouldn't be the wisest move. You could just imagine it:

'Hey Son, did you have a good week away?' Who? That man in the kitchen with a beer watching football? Why that's your new dad, go give him a hug.'

So she was due here in an hour but was thinking maybe it wasn't the best idea and maybe she should just come around mine later instead. But I couldn't do that without it sounding like I was bottling it, which of course, I would have been. No, I grabbed Lucy and explained the situation.

She was, as I'd expected really, all good with it. Don't suppose she really has too much of a leg to stand on. She took the piss a bit about me taking so long to finally meet someone and said she was looking forward to meeting her. I told her that's great but please don't try and fuck her. She laughed and flashed her wedding ring at me saying she's taken. Oh how I enjoyed sex banter with this weirdo.

Kate showed up, looking extremely pretty in a dress that screamed sexy step mum without looking too sexy. I think there's a compliment there somewhere. She looked fit and sensible but with an edge. Good stuff.

I introduced her to everyone I knew at the party, which wasn't all that many as it goes, most of the parents from play group I didn't really know, the ones I knew a little sort of just threw their kids in and scarpered to the nearby shops. She got on with everyone and I got the thumbs up from Bates and Yvonne. Luckily Stuart and Paul weren't here to mess things up in their own ways.

Now I was going to introduce her to the most important lady in my life, no, not Margot Robbie. I grabbed up Grace. I had to be quick, she was extremely busy. Those slides need to be slid on. "Grace," I started. "I want you to meet daddy's friend, this is Kate."

"Hi," She grinned with a wave.

"Hi to you Grace," Kate swooned. "Happy birthday, aren't you just a little beauty?"

"No, I'm two!"

"Yes you are and I've got you a little present, here you go." Kate handed a box wrapped in Bing-themed wrapping paper, good start. Bing. Another little fucker she loved and I loathed.

"Fanks," Grace said grabbing it, I put her down and she opened it. It was a talking Peppa Pig toy. Fucking great.

"Wow, fanks, I love him!" She gave Kate a hug. And she ran off. Ah two year olds. Easy.

I looked at Kate as I was picking up the new toy's now empty box and told her she was dead.

"She is adorable, and she clearly loves you."

"Well what can I say? I'm mentally about two so we are a good team."

"Just get ready for the terrible twos!"

Shit yeah, why was everyone mentioning this. Could they be *that* bad?

The rest of the party went well, I kept my attention on Grace whilst making sure Kate was having fun. It was coming to an end with a little bit of dancing. I needed to get my dance in with her but it would be proper weird doing it here at *Toddlers Kingdom*. I'd asked people back to the house already anyway. Quick stop at the off licence and we were back at mine. Being all smooth I told Kate I had a spare toothbrush, just like the Saint I thought. She told me she'd brought her own. Definitely had one to hold onto here.

"Bit presumptuous," I joked, literally beaming from ear to ear. How perfect was the day. My little baby was turning into a real little girl and I had a beautiful woman here with a bag with a toothbrush and a pair of knickers in because she wanted to stay with me.

It was approaching 7pm and Grace was flaking as expected. I Got All The Time In The World on and grabbed her for our dance. Same as a year ago. This time with a few more people watching. I really hoped it didn't look turdy. But I think I noticed Kate looking at us like I was one of the greatest people alive. And Grace was holding me tight. Until I put her down and the dance turned into a full on baby bop dance off.

The next morning Grace slept in so Kate and I were up and having breakfast when she awoke. I went and got her and brought her downstairs. She was holding her Peppa Pig toy. Well done Kate, think it was her favourite present. Oddly enough, Kate was mine.

The next few months were great. Kate was a full on part of our lives, She had a key to mine and would spend the time with us when Connor was with his dad, normally one night in the week and most weekends. I'd met Connor, so had Grace and he was a sweet kid. As for the dad, who I'd also met as he wanted to 'approve' me, he was sure to let me know just how tough he was. Within five minutes of meeting him, he asked me to help him get a box from the boot of his car, I couldn't say no. When we got there it was a smallish, light box but on top of it was an army beret.

"Sorry," he said. "That's mine, don't know how that got on there."

I do, you put it on there you soft prick. He'd also told me he had to kill rabbits when in the army. Watch out. Turned out he'd only lasted eight months in the army but let's not let that ruin a hard-nut in full swing.

We'd been seeing each other for about eight months. I suppose approaching a year together. Anniversaries were always going to be easy to remember, a week before Grace's birthday. Ah Grace.

What a character she was really turning into. Terrible two's yeah sure, meltdowns and tantrums, but I just couldn't help but laugh. She used the word 'No' with incredible determination sometimes, obviously folding every time you said 'but if you do this you can *then* do that'. Potty training was fun. Luckily I had hardwood flooring throughout downstairs otherwise the carpets would have been beyond hope of saving. It was actually Kate who finally got it cracked. We made the upstairs toilet the 'girls' toilet and that was that. Like a switch had been flicked, she no longer wanted nappies. Even through the night she didn't wear them anymore. 'Dad (not even daddy now sometimes) *big* girls don't need a nappy even at night'. She sounded like that twat Peppa Pig but I let it go. She was two and half going on fifteen. She even got up from the sofa one evening to say that she was going to the bathroom and would Kate like to join her. God only knows where she would get some of her sayings from. 'Be right with you' 'That would be great' and 'Is that wise?' were just a few. Also everything was simply divided by either a girl's one or a boy's one. Potatoes and veg she'd eat if you told her they were girl ones. Everything that was pink she'd want. Everything that wasn't pink but she wanted, had to be found in pink. Of course the most awkward occasion was as I was coming out of the shower and she was in my bedroom, showing Kate her new dance, when she spotted, not for the first time, my erm, appendage.

"What *is* that Daddy?"

"I've told you before Princess, it's my boy bits."

"I want one. I want one for Christmas. And I want a pink one."

Good luck with that. I always thought I'd tell any daughter of mine to run a mile from these things, all her life. But I thought she will probably get that instruction from her mums.

It was fast approaching her third birthday and the last eighteen months we'd attacked and conquered: talking, walking, weeing, pooing, monsters, Gruffalos and my toughest, hair styles. When she was a couple of months old I'd bought one of those heads you practice on if you're a trainee hairdresser, to practice just simple things like bunches and ponytails. Simple? I wasn't so sure. Other mums would still look twice when I dropped her at nursery and she'd always come home with nice hair. I often wondered if they did it the second I left or at least waited until it actually needed doing again. But it wasn't a big problem. Especially as she'd now banned me from doing it, 'Kate can do it now thanks Dad,' she'd often say.

Her third birthday was now here and the party was at Lucy and Syd's, which I didn't mind as it was far less for me to sort and I could concentrate on having a good time and making sure Grace was. And Kate. I'd surprised Kate earlier in the week for our anniversary and we were booked for a weekend in Bruge the following weekend. No Connor and no Grace, I did say we could perhaps book a week in the summer somewhere for all four of us.

I was in the good books that's for sure. She'd got me a meal at Tom Kerridge's restaurant in a couple of weeks, good chance for me to compare my pies to his!

The house was completely decked out in Hello Kitty. As horrendous as it was, Grace loved it. They'd hired three Princesses to be there (probably for *them* to gawp at) and got outside caterers to do the food. They told me it was £600 for the food; I told them I'd have done it for £400 and much better. But these two were apparently flying high in their respective jobs so whatever they wanted to spend then why not. I liked the fact that Grace should be secure financially through her life and it didn't just fall on me, which was a good thing as my work had definitely taken a hit since Grace was born. Not that I cared, I was loving it.

My friends came to the party, which was aimed at adults too as there was a lot of booze there. I was off duty tonight as Grace was staying here so I spent quite a bit of time with them, listening to the madness. I walked in on Paul responding to being asked, "What rhymes with orange?"

"No it doesn't," was his, I'd like to say clever response, but I knew better. He was a lovely bloke Paul but he didn't help himself sometimes. I often thought that he just needs a young lady in his life. One that's thicker than him. I thought I'd found such a person at this party. She was one of Syd's friends so thought I'd best sound her out about whether she, well, preferred sausage or taco. Turns out, straight as they come. And pretty damn dumb. This could be magic.

She'd already said 'fravourite' to me four or five times, 'chimley' instead of chimney and talked about 'chester draws'. Are they draws from Chester I'd asked. I suppose they're easy things to miss pronounce and plenty of people do but she'd also told me that at her work she has to be 'grammically perfect'. 'Grammatically,' I gently corrected before looking for a way of getting these two in the same room. I told a story about when I was younger, I'd gone over the handlebars of my bike on a busy road and landed on my head and she gasped and said, "Did you die?"

"No." I left to get a beer and said I'd be back. Not without Paul I wouldn't be.

As I got to the kitchen Stuart was there. He'd had to nip off to drop something home and actually borrowed Kate's car. I asked if everything was okay and he said all was good. "Why does she have that thing around her steering wheel? It makes the wheel really thick and massive," he said to me.

"I don't know mate, why was it a problem?"

"Nah, I took it off but can't get it back on again."

"Took it off?! Why bother, you drove about five miles in it."

"I know, but when you turned right it was like trying to give an anaconda a Chinese burn, I couldn't be dealing with it. Anyway I reckon she only likes it on there so she can feel something substantial in her hands every so often after being with you for a year," he said, taking the sausage roll out of my hand and hitting me on the arm and walking off.

"Wanker!" was the best I had to shout after him.

"Dad," it was Grace, right next to me which I hadn't seen. "What's a wanker?"

Brilliant. "Nothing Princess, just a fun name I call Uncle Stuart every so often."

The rest of the afternoon was actually pretty great. Grace loved every minute of it and Paul was still chatting to this girl I introduced him to, Debbie I think. I dreaded to think what about but did over-hear her asking him if Henry VIII was famous for being the Prime Minister during World War One or Two. I didn't hear his answer but he'd probably pick one and try and sound like a wise old owl.

It was time for 'our dance' I'd call it and Grace did too, which melted me. Again it was a bit strange, the music changing from the Frozen soundtrack to Louis Armstrong but most people knew the coo now, which meant more people watched. Hopefully it was because it was crazy sweet and not just to laugh at me.

Again, it was one of my favourite moments of the year. She always held on with a real good hug and then showed me all her new moves she'd picked up. The song finished and we stopped and walked off, Stuart stopped Grace and said, "Good dance moves Gracie Goo, you'll be on the stage one day, mark my words."

"Thanks wanker," she returned.

EIGHT

Grace being three was pretty uneventful for the most part. It will always be one of my favourite ages though as she just entertained me all the time, whether it was on purpose or not, it was all lovely. I was watching her grow up right in front of my eyes, and she was desperate to grow up. She'd have her 'baby' that she'd look after like it was real, she talked on the phone to her mum with the phone wedged between her ear and shoulder whilst checking her nails and walking round saying 'sure' and 'yeah, why not'. It was pure entertainment. The rest of the time I couldn't even begin to try and write the other things that made me laugh. It was a case of you had to be there. And luckily for me, I was and it will always be in my memory bank.

Kate and I were getting on great, Connor even seemed to quite like me, surely it wouldn't last. He was nearly nine and already showing signs of teenage moodiness. They hadn't moved in with me but I knew it would happen soon. We'd discussed it and the stumbling block was Connor. I had a third bedroom but it was quite small. Connor was a growing lad and probably needed more room but I wasn't going to move Grace out of her room, especially as Connor was with his dad a few times a week. I know Grace was with her mum(s) three, sometimes four, nights a week but I just didn't want to do it! Plus, I'm pretty sure Grace wouldn't want to move, she loved her bedroom and anyway she had to share her room with her baby. Yep, she had a cot, changing station, even a little doll wardrobe. I wasn't sure how cute this still was or if it was bordering on a future serial killer situation. I'm joking, it was very sweet. Especially when she told her off, wagging her finger and putting her on the naughty step.

Grace turned four, again there was a bit of a party. All went well. It was at the local play centre again. I thought this could be the last one at a place like this, she'd already told me it was for babies really, but she had a good time as expected, no matter if she thought it wasn't grown up enough. "Next year I want to go ice skating, go cinema and out for dinner," she told me. Brat.

There was no after party this time, Lucy and Syd were both snowed under at work apparently and we didn't open it up to friends. I had Bates and Yvonne coming round as well as Paul who was bringing Debbie, yep they'd hit it off last year and were going strong. Probably helping each other to walk and talk at the same time or something. Stuart was coming and asked if he could bring his latest girlfriend, I hadn't met her but said it was fine. CK came with Miss America as we called her, as all she seemed to talk about was how she missed America. *Well move back there then,* Stuart said to her once.

We were back from the party around 4pm and Kate and Grace went off to sort her new presents and do each other's hair or something whilst I got on with making pies. I was making a rustic ham, potato and pea pie and a venison and stout pie. My mate was a butcher and always sorted me out. They were gorgeous even if I do say so myself. Of course Stuart's friend was a vegetarian which I should have asked. *'Not when you're chowing down on my ol' fella you're not,'* he'd delightfully said at the table. Luckily, as always I'd done plenty of veg and I had a bit of salmon in so she had that with a couple of potato options. Mash and roasties. She polished off quite a few roasties, I didn't realise until the next day when Kate asked how I'd done them and we realised it was in duck fat. Oh well, what you don't know won't hurt.

Just before we were going to eat I was settling Grace ready for bed when she said, "What about our dance daddy?"

Blimey, can't believe I'd forgotten. And I noticed I was daddy not dad, always so much more sweet to hear. "Corr, well remembered Princess, I'd almost forgotten about that!"

"Erm, you completely forgot about it daddy, good job I'm here isn't it?"

"In so many ways sweetpea, come on, let's do it!" So downstairs we went. I gladly interrupted the Ed Sheerin playlist somebody had put on and started our Louis Armstrong song. We just danced to it in the kitchen, this time though Grace started on her feet and we danced and towards the end I picked her up for my squeeze and hug. She told me she loved me and I asked if she loved me more than chocolate. "Some chocolate," was her answer.

She said good night to everyone and I took her up to bed. I was tucking her in and she told me she actually loved me more than ALL chocolate. Even Kinder Eggs.

I went back downstairs to our attempted sophisticated dinner. That would be impossible to do with Stuart and Paul there. And as it turned out, Debbie. She was lovely but she told us this story about when she lived in America. And I think it just about summed her up.

"So," she was saying, "I was in New York, I wonder if there was ever an old York?" She asked almost to herself, shrugged and giggled a bit and carried on. "Yeah, sorry. So I was in New York and my rent was so high and my wages weren't so I had to start looking for somewhere else to live. I spotted an ad in the paper and it said, '*Room to let. Only $90p/w but Lighthouse keeping involved.*' So I was like, ooh, I don't know anything about lighthouses so did a bit of research. I always remembered that one in Fraggle Rock and thought I'd quite like that. What's not to like, sea view, I could get a dog. Thought it'd be interesting. So I responded and got invited to go for a chat. I was with the chap for nearly an hour when I finally asked where is it and when can I see the lighthouse. Well, he looked at me like some crazy lady. Turns out the ad said '*Light house-keeping involved*' as in I had to help keep the whole place clean and we were actually in the place that was for rent. I felt like such an idiot!"

Laughter from around the table as it was a great story. But she was genuinely perplexed. All this did was start more crazy stories around the table. Stuart started one that we, his friends had heard a few times before but I knew the women around the table might not have so I kept quiet. Even though it was definitely bullshit. If not, just mental.

"Yeah, that's what I said, I was born twice," he was saying.

"What do you mean, born twice?!" Kate asked before emptying and refilling her wine glass, and topping mine up. Marry me I thought.

"Exactly that, my mum told me. She was getting rushed in to hospital in an ambulance. I was six weeks early you see."

"Ah. You've been arriving early since then have you? Explains it," His new girlfriend Kelly said. This brought a lot of laughs. We liked her.

"Very funny! Just for that I'm not putting out later!" She fist bumped herself. "Anyway yeah, so my mum was in the back of the ambulance and I was coming out there and then. She pushed and my head came out. Then the ambulance hit a speed bump or pothole or something and my head went back in."

"Oh shut up," Said Debbie. "That's impossible."

"Nope, god's honest truth. So she pushed me back out and there you go. I reckon I'm the only man since Jesus to be born twice."

"He wasn't born twice," Bates said

"Well even better. I'm the only man ever then."

This wasn't my favourite Stuart story and egged him on to tell everyone about when he lost his virginity. Now I knew me and Bates were the only one who knew this story. Don't even think Paul and CK knew.

"No way," he said, but I could see he wanted to. He finished his wine and topped it up again and said, "Okay then," loving his chance to take centre stage.

"Well, I was fifteen and my mum and dad had to go to Holland for work. They owned a shoe shop and went to sort out some new stock.

"Clogs?" Paul asked

"No, not fucking clogs," Stuart said.

"Anyway, it was Amsterdam and I thought I'd jump on this and ask to come. They used to take me kicking and screaming to these things but I was younger then. I mean, how many twelve year olds want to go to Milan and that. So I got the okay and was planning to get as much weed in me as possible. But then I thought I could get rid of this millstone around my neck. I'd had a couple of girlfriends but hadn't got past third base yet."

"Because they were always about eleven years old," Paul chipped in again.

"So," Stuart continued, ignoring him, "I thought I'd get it done and rack up a ton of experience in doing it. I took myself off down to the red-light district. Actually had to ask a couple for directions, no google maps back then you know. It was funny because I asked an old married couple and as the wife said she didn't know, the bloke was already pointing the way. Schoolboy error right there I thought. So anyway, I mooched around a bit looking at the girls in the windows until I decided which one I wanted, rang the doorbell and in I went. Before I could point to the window girl this huge black woman grabbed my arm and led me upstairs to a room behind a skanky curtain. She looked like that chef, Rustie Lee, if you remember her?"

I don't think many did but hey ho.

"She tells me it's like 50 quid or whatever and strips off."

"£50 hey? Bargain," said CK.

"Then," Stuart continued, "she looks at me and tells me I need to wash my old boy in the sink over there."

"Wait," Paul interrupted, "you had to wash your dad in the sink? Why was he even with you?"

Everyone looked at him, my head dropped into my hands. "No you fucking inbred! Not my dad you moron. My Johnson, dick, penis, knob. Whatever you want to call it. Jesus Christ. Wash my old boy in… Fucking hell, why would I need to wash my dad in a sink?"

"Oh right, yeah," to be fair, even Paul looked a bit embarrassed with that one.

"Anyway. I rattled the headboard of the Dutch Tessa Sanderson for a few minutes and it was done. I was a man."

I didn't think that story would ever be the same again after that. The 'Paul' factor.

Grace, now that she was four, was to start school in the following September. She was born in December so she'd be fairly old for her year and I think she was more than ready. But was I?

She was unbelievably cute in her uniform but already looking too old too quickly for my liking, but what could be done about that? Nothing. I had to embrace it and I did with enormous pride and satisfaction at what a lovely girl she was.

We all took her in on that first morning. I brought Kate with me, Syd and Lucy brought Iris. Grace loved the fact we all were there. It was only a half day but all five of us picked her up too. Luckily it was an evening she was with me, so all six of us went for ice-cream before we took her home. She said she enjoyed school and already had three best friends. If they were anything like mine I'd move her to a different school! It was good she liked school but I also didn't have the heart to tell her she had fourteen years minimum left at it.

Her being four and starting school quickly meant she was turning five. No party for her, just took her and nine of her 'besties' to the cinema and ice skating, then Pizza Hut. She had them sleepover too, that was a nightmare but Kate took control of it. Oh yeah, Kate and Connor had moved in and things were good. I got my dance in with Grace but also had to dance with her friends for about an hour after to god knows what type of music it was until Kate came and saved me. She spent the evening telling fairy tales and snacking on rubbish until well past midnight when the final friend fell asleep. Connor, who was now 10, sat with me watching a movie but we both flaked at about 9pm. It was a good day but I was tired!

One evening, which summed us up, Kate and I were finishing up watching a 'who done it' on TV and when it finished she asked, "Well how did the police know it was him that killed the dead bloke?"

"Did you see that after he was stabbed, he crawled to the garden and grabbed a bit of basil and clenched it in his fist so the detective finally realised it was a clue and it was the blokes Uncle Basil that did it, because he was holding a bit of basil. Very clever," I told her.

"Oh," she said and then carried on. "Good job it wasn't his Uncle Dick then wasn't it!"

The following couple of years Grace excelled at absolutely everything. She was intelligent, funny, caring and sweet. Time just zipped by, at her school I was very proud of how all the parents evenings went, the talent shows and the nativities. Basically just chuffed to bits about how she was turning out. Grace always seemed to be a central part in a lot of lives. She was popular, not just with kids and parents at her school but at all the clubs she was in. Even my mates got advice from her! Stuart even 'borrowed' her a couple of times to go shopping. She'd play the delightful niece if he chatted up any women and in return he'd buy her a present at the end of the day. She was a businesswoman at seven years old. I don't know where she got it from! Certainly wasn't me. My life was just about perfect. It was in the November, not long before Grace was due to turn eight that my life got flipped well and truly on its fucking head.

Turned out Grace wasn't the only one doing well in life. So was Lucy. She called me up and asked if we could meet up. It was at her house around midday and Grace was at school. I actually thought it might be because she was broody and it would be for a sperm donation via a turkey baster. Not so weirdly, I was well wide of the mark.

"I've been promoted at work," straight to the point like always.

"That's great," I replied. "You just got me here to brag then?"

"My new role isn't local," she continued. "It's in Singapore."

NINE

The drive home was, to put it mildly, weird. I actually pulled over twice to run through things in my head again. Lucy said Singapore and I think I laughed. Yeah, I did and then said something lame like *'that's one hell of a commute'*. But Lucy was far from smiling. She went on to explain how her company wanted her to head up their new office in Singapore from February. And she was doing it. Just like that. Of course at this point I'm thinking, *'how the hell can you even think about leaving your daughter'*.

Silly me.

"Okay," I said to her and sat down. "Congratulations I guess is the right thing to say. What's Syd said?"

"She's over the moon."

Must be a big lesbian community over there then. A rubbish one though because don't they have small boobs? What's the point in being a lesbian if you don't get to play with big knockers at least? Why the fuck was I concentrating on this?!

"Okay, well sounds like the future for you is changing. And for me. What's the plan for coming back to see Grace and all that?"

"She's coming," she whispered.

"Coming where? She's not moving to Singapore, you do know that don't you?"

"I'm so sorry to do this but, yes, she is. I'm her mother."

"I don't give a flying fuck if you're her Siamese fucking twin you're not taking her away from me. Especially Singapore?! Not local you said. Jesus. What's that? About 5000 miles away?! I thought you were going to say London, or something. Fucking Singa-fucking-pore?" I remember actually thinking how many f-bombs I was dropping. And thinking it wasn't enough.

"Let's not make this difficult hey?" she said.

That's when I lost it completely. I obviously don't mean in an 'attacking her' way. But I can't even remember what I'd yelled. Syd had by this point returned and got me to leave. I wasn't messing with that brick shithouse. Can you hit the manly lesbian or is it still hitting a woman? I wasn't sure. Not that I'd dare.

I got in my car and sped off. *Let's not make this difficult hey.* I was saying it back to myself the same way she had said it to me. In the patronising fuckwit tone she often used. Who did she think she was? One thing was certain. No way was Grace going.

I obviously didn't go back into work that afternoon. I couldn't even sit down at home. I was still fuming. Where did I actually stand legally on this situation? Bates worked for a law firm, I'll have to speak to him but not before Kate. I phoned her, still freaking out about it. She said she was coming home so I waited.

She was as shocked and as distraught as I was. We got onto Bates who gave me the number for a family lawyer. After speaking to him for about half an hour I booked a meeting with him on Monday and that weekend was the longest of my life. And to make matters worse, it was only ten days until Grace's birthday. Grace, poor poor Grace. She was going to get caught in the middle of all this.

On the Monday I met with Michael Holness. He told me, in short, that I have a decent say in matters these days, especially as I'm on the birth certificate. Thank god I went with her that day. I had parental responsibility. Of course, as I'm working on my side of things, Lucy had her company's lawyer working on her's. I'm still not sure what she exactly did for a living but she must be good because they really wanted her for this gig. And they were powerful.

The next month was horrible. I spent half my time shouting at Lucy and Syd and half my time begging them not to do this. My relationship with Kate was changing as well and not for the better, completely down to me but I was just not in a happy place. Work had also been put to one side which was not going unnoticed. My savings were quickly vanishing towards this lawyer too.

Things had got so bad during this time that Grace had to have separate birthday parties. I don't think she particularly minded that but asked a lot of questions about what was going on. As I said, she was a bright girl and she knew something was wrong. Very wrong.

Syd, to be fair, acted as a go between for a lot of it. Not that I cared what she had to say, just as long as she listened to me. She was obviously sympathetic but I also knew where her loyalty was and understood that. It was the New Year and already the 'move' was pushed back to Easter, I thought it was a little victory. But it was only so the court date could be met. This had gone that far.

Grace had been told what was going on, I wasn't telling her but Lucy and Syd did. She didn't quite understand what it meant but she seemed happy to be going on a plane again. I didn't have the heart to say it might mean not seeing daddy for months at a time, I wanted to break down and cry every time I thought about it.

It was late March, Grace was eight and we were nearing the court hearing. Michael Holness had been good, expensive but hopefully worth it and he was confident. Kate was really good, we'd come through a bit of a sticky patch not surprisingly but she was lots of help with my down periods. I thought maybe this might actually work out okay for me. Then I got called into work. And got fired.

I couldn't believe it. Actually I could because I'd been rubbish. Certainly over the last three or four months. But as my boss, ex-boss I should say, explained, I'd been getting worse since having Grace. I had, but he had no right to say that to me and I was actually glad to be out of there if he thought I'd apologise for prioritising my daughter for eight years. But the timing couldn't be worse. I even asked if they could sack me a month later but got told to basically fuck off. I was thirty-four years old with no job and about to go to court to win my daughter. How did things end up like this?

I told my lawyer and he thought I was joking. That can't be good. I also told Syd who in turn told Lucy and thought she'd really push this newly found advantage. She, to my surprise, came round the next day and we had our first normal, adult conversation for months.

She said to me that there's an option to explore where her company would pay for me three return flights a year, they'd actually be for Lucy but she said she had no plans in coming back and forth and the company said they can be used by me. She said I can feel free to stay with them rather than have to pay for a hotel. Now I knew Singapore was expensive but the thought of hearing them two going at it on a nightly basis? I thought I'd fork out for digs. She also suggested I get a job and a place out there. That wasn't an option unfortunately. When I was eighteen I was arrested for getting caught out in a brawl outside a nightclub. I actually didn't do anything but a friend did. He was on his third strike and I took the fall for him. I got a criminal record for it and that right there took away any chance of getting a full-time Visa in Singapore, which was very strict. Idiot. And of course there was Kate and Connor. Kate couldn't leave Connor and his dad would never budge.

What was I going to do? Three flights a year. I could perhaps pay for three as well. Even if I got a job that would let me take that much time off, would I be able to afford it? I'd want two weeks each time but I'm never getting twelve weeks off. And twelve weeks out of fifty-two..? That leaves forty weeks a year not seeing Grace. But my chances of keeping her had apparently gone. I was unemployed, unmarried and broke and was up against a married, well-off, high flying, happy gay couple.

I was advised to still take the court option as you never knew which way the judge would lean.

———————————

The day was here and I was the most nervous I'd ever been. And it didn't go well. The fact of the money, opportunity, lifestyle and that Syd was going to be a stay at home parent swung it their way. They were ordered to pay for two return flights throughout a year and that was that. My life was over, just like that.

I'm not ashamed to say I broke down in the courtroom. Howling and screaming before anger took over and I started aiming my anger at these horrible bastards that had ripped out my heart. I was pinned down by my friends and security and informed this was not helping my case. Case? How was keeping my daughter a case?

I don't remember getting home that afternoon but went straight to bed. Throughout the night I was hatching plans on what to do. Firstly I was going to buy a batman outfit and climb the tallest building I could find. I thought maybe I'll fly Grace off to the Caribbean and not come back. But I didn't have any money left. To make matters worse they were going in nine days. Lucy, because of my outburst in court, and I think she was probably right to worry about me being a flight risk, said that she didn't want me left alone with Grace at all. This was ridiculous. Nine days left and I would have to have dinner with Iris or someone. I don't think I'd ever hated anyone in my life before, but I actually hated Lucy. Oddly enough she'd given me the greatest thing in my life but I hated her because now she was tearing it away.

I also had to get a job. Kate said to me about having a baby. I should have loved her more for this but I didn't. It actually wound me up and turned into a row. "It's not a fucking sofa you know," I said rather unfairly. "I don't want to just replace Grace with a new one" It was harsh but I was not a happy person. I knew she meant well but she ended up storming off.

The next nine days I had to make the best nine days of my life but I had a feeling they would be the worst. I had to apologise to Kate as soon as possible; she would want to spend as much time with Grace too. How she wasn't a factor in Grace staying in England I'll never know. I should have got married to her! Probably not the best reason I suppose.

The nine days went ridiculously quickly. Kate understood my reaction after a bit of a chat but I had to promise to stay positive. That wasn't going to be easy but I said that I would certainly try my best. Grace didn't sleep at mine the first three nights as Lucy was being a real prick. I had her through the days each time until around 7pm and then she would be picked up by Syd. It's hard to describe the feeling I had at the time. Awful is an understatement. It was nearing a point where I felt sorry for Grace to be with me because I was so upset all the time. I thought I hid it pretty well from her but on the third day she asked me why I kept taking myself off to the bedroom and that she'd heard me crying in the bathroom a couple of times. I tried to claim I was just struggling to poo and it was painful but she didn't buy it. She told me everything would be okay and we can talk every night once she's gone and she was going to be fine.

She was such a smart girl but she didn't realise that although talking will be good, it's not enough for me. Even facetime would still leave me missing so much of her life. It was when she left on day three, as I was calling it, day three of nine, I phoned Lucy and asked to meet. I wanted her for these last six days, twenty-four hours on each of them. Grace not Lucy obviously.

I met Lucy at the pub later that evening and laid out what I wanted and basically pleaded.

"I know what you're saying, believe me but I just don't trust you to not run off with her," she explained.

"I've got no money to sodding run off, this has cleaned me out!"

"Well I told you we should have sorted it between ourselves."

I don't know what she thought she was getting at but she was probably right in a strange way, I'd have actually ended up with an extra flight and about £15,000 left in my account.

"I understand that but what if it was the other way around, what would you have done?" I countered.

"That's just hypothetical and won't get us anywhere"

I knew the answer but didn't push it. There are going to be bigger battles to win.

"Can you please just trust me one last time, I need to see her as much as possible, I want to be the one to bring her to the airport and I want her from tomorrow until then. Please?"

"Okay, I'm not completely heartless and I know what a good dad you are. And she will be missing you too so okay. You get her tomorrow but I want her back on Thursday evening. We leave Friday morning but I'm not running that risk of you not turning up so I'll take her but obviously you can meet us at the airport to say goodbye. That fair?"

Fair?! What the fuck was fair about any of this? I couldn't say this despite wanting to absolutely erupt. I bit my tongue and said okay. *Okay you fucking heart-wrecking, twat-licking whore of a dog,* is what I actually wanted to say. But didn't.

I drove home planning on what to do with Grace. These last few days I wanted to count. I thought about a party but didn't want to share her.

I didn't actually let her out of my sight when we were awake, I took her wherever she wanted to go, spoiled her rotten and I didn't care. I lay next to her when she was going to sleep and then went to bed and cried myself to sleep each night.

On the Wednesday after Grace was asleep there was a knock at the door and it was Syd. She was here to, as it seemed, fight my corner. Or at least try and help me out in any way she could. And I really appreciated it. She said she'd offer to fly Grace back herself every year. It wasn't brilliant but it was the best I could expect. And I appreciated the gesture.

On the Thursday, my last whole day with Grace was horrible. I tried staying positive with her as much as possible but my stomach was upside down, my brain had a constant fog and my heart felt ripped in half. My friends came around mine to say their goodbyes to her. Paul popped in to say goodbye but looked more upset at me being upset. Then Bates' came and Yvonne looked like she'd never let go of Grace and just kept saying, "There must be something we can do". *'If only,'* was my general response. Stuart was round for the longest and was by far the most upset. I don't think I'd ever seen him this upset. Even when he found out he had genital warts. He hugged Grace goodbye again and had to leave without stopping or looking at me. He text later to say sorry about that. But he didn't need to.

We ate dinner, just me, Grace and Kate. Connor was at his dad's. We had mac and cheese with pink ice cream for pudding, all at Grace's request obviously. It felt like my last meal on death row. But I'd have had pie if that was ever the case, which it might have been the way I was feeling about a certain someone for doing this to me. And of course, if we lived in one of the twenty-nine states in America that had the death penalty.

Grace was also subdued the whole evening. The reality had hit her and she too was struggling. It was horrible to see. I knew she'd be good tomorrow with the plane journey and the general excitement of it all but I didn't like her like this. I let her stay up until 11pm because I didn't want her going to bed and also to make sure she was grumpy tomorrow for a day of travelling with them.

We talked a lot of the evening in between me nipping off to howl into a tea towel in the kitchen. She told me how much she loved me as I did her. Just before bed I put on Louis Armstrong and we danced. We didn't dance the way we would for her birthday. She sort of just stood and I was on my knees and we just hugged with a little bit of swaying.

Kate went off to do something in the kitchen, I think as she is so nice, to give us our moment. It was the first time this song had made me so sad but will also fill me with many great memories. It was our song and always would be. She was my girl and always would be.

EVERY STEP OF THE WAY WILL FIND US

WITH ALL THE CARES OF THE WORLD FAR BEHIND US..

WE HAVE ALL THE TIME IN THE WORLD

JUST FOR LOVE

NOTHING MORE, NOTHING LESS

ONLY LOVE...

TEN

It had been a month since Grace had gone. I'd facetimed her every single day, there was seven hours difference, it'll be eight in the winter, so it was quite important to get the times right and we settled on 7pm her time and 12 noon for me so she could fill me in on her day. She was enjoying it, which was, I suppose, the most important thing. I was flying out there with Kate the next day. A month seemed like a lifetime and as you can imagine I was rather excited.

The airport a month earlier had been horrible. The only way I could process it was to pretend I was just waving her off for a week. I got home and instantly got our flights sorted. I'd have gone the week after but thought I'd best let them settle a bit. The rest of that day is just a blur. My head had gone and I just wanted to lie in bed and cry. Which I did.

After that first weekend, I went out and got a job. Just driving for a courier firm. I told myself, and Kate, that it was just while I kept looking properly but secretly I was just thinking I'd be better just getting jobs I didn't care about and could leave, or be sacked every time I was going to see Grace. To be fair I didn't actually mind it. Just out and about driving and speaking to a few bored and flirty housewives. I told them when I got the job I was away for these two weeks which they honoured. Just as well because I'd have walked out there and then.

So we were flying out the next evening. I'd been packed a week ready to go. But tonight we had to go to Paul's for dinner. I say had to, I was looking forward to it. All my friends had been brilliant trying to keep my spirits up, as was Kate.

We arrived at Paul's, or Paul and Debbie's I suppose now as she had moved in. The dinner party was so they could tell us *'some exciting news'* which we assumed would be an engagement announcement.

Kate and I were the last to arrive. Stuart was there, a little drunk and a lot single. He'd split up with his latest one but already had his sights on someone else and required Yvonne to put in a good word. We all sat around the table and ate and drank wine. We only briefly talked about Grace; I would happily talk about her all the time but also was wary about *only* talking about her. Then Paul started to tell us the news.

"Thanks for coming everyone and me and Debbie have got some news..."

"We are pregnant!" they said in a rehearsed unison.

Well, we weren't expecting that. I'm surprised they knew where to put it during sex but we all congratulated them and I was really, really happy for them. I'd best let him know he should get married and hide Debbie's passport straight away!

Dinner, food wise, was okay I'd say at best, if I was being my food-snob self. We finished and chatted around the table. Debbie and Paul were filling us in over how they found out the news.

"Well, I hadn't you know, had a period for like, ages and ages. And my boobs were hurting," Debbie said whilst grabbing her own boobs.

"So I joked maybe you're Keith Cheggers," Paul chipped in.

"Well I suddenly thought, yeah maybe I am and sent Paul off to get a test."

"So, off I went," Paul continued, like they were like some kind of double act. Had this actually been rehearsed?! "But when I got to Tesco there were like, a hundred different types and I didn't know what was best. So I just grabbed three of them and brought them back!"

"Well," back to Debbie (and every sentence started with a well), "I was holding my pee pee in because I was proper desperate but he got back and I pee'd on all three of them and we sat and waited."

"Then after a minute or so, they all came through as positive!" Paul said with visible glee. "Tell them what you said though babe."

"Shut up," Debbie said, more like shut aaaaapp the way she said it. "Well," she giggled and continued, "I was in like shock and like didn't know what to say. But I looked at Paul and said, and I don't know why I said it, oh my god, all three have come back positive! How are we going to raise three kids? Didn't I?!" and she and Paul burst out laughing. It was funny, but I couldn't help but think this poor kid had no chance!

But we were all delighted for them. Stuart, who had been fairly quiet through the night started going on about a girl he liked down at the coffee shop in town. Yvonne had shot him down over her mate which might be why he was quiet. We all could picture the girl at the coffee shop and she wasn't that pretty if we were being honest, and harsh. But for Stuart, she was definitely below his usual standards. Maybe age was catching up with him but he was adamant she was the next cab off the rank.

"Honestly," he started, "if I have to have one more cup of coffee this week I'm going to need peeling off the ceiling. I'm in there about four times a day!"

"Sad," said Paul. "You sad sad man."

"Alright pal. We can't all find our perfect match and when delivering news act like Tweedledum and tweedledumber," he bit back.

"But I thought you liked my mate Laura?!" Said Yvonne

"Irons in fires love, irons in fires."

"Or if you throw shit at a wall, a bit will stick," she replied.

"Anyway, I think I'll go for coffee Carrie, I think she's stunning."

"If you think she's stunning you should see one of my friends, Ellie," said Kate.

"Oh yeah, she a bit of a stunner then?"

"No…. She's an optician."

Today was the day. Airport day and off to see my Grace! I didn't sleep much despite the wine. I was just too excited. And I thought maybe I'd sleep on the plane. It was thirteen hours so I'd better bloody sleep.

The taxi arrived and Kate had packed to clothe the whole of Singapore I think.

"We have a 30lb limit on the cases you know," I said.

"No, *WE* have 60lbs, yours has a pair of shorts and flip-flops. I'm just using your quota too," I guess she actually made sense!

We got to the airport in good time only to find the plane was delayed. Obviously. It was only an hour and once we got on the plane the pilot said he hoped to make up the time. I actually thought that if they can make up an hour why, when they take off on time, did they not land an hour early? But now wasn't the time to worry about aeronautical dilemmas. I was going to see my baby!

The plane journey was okay; we chatted, ate, had little naps, watched films and had a little drink. I could get used to this. Looked like I might have to anyway! Kate didn't take me up on the mile high club offer though. I ordered her another gin & tonic and thought I'd ask again after that. Still a no. We landed in Singapore at around 4pm local time, so that was 9am back home. I should have been shattered but was buzzing too much to see Grace. Syd said she'd arranged a taxi to pick us up and would be waiting with a sign once we were through the very strict customs. Jesus was it strict, good thing I guess but I didn't know who to look at or whether to smile, look aloof or what. In those instances no matter what, you do you look like you're trying to hide the fact you have a kilo of cocaine up your bum. God knows why anybody would try and smuggle drugs into Singapore though, even the pilot warned us on landing that any drugs found and it's the death penalty! Even chewing gum here meant potential jail time. So here I was in this queue, looking like I had gum as I was chewing my lip with nerves and scratching my arse like it had something foreign in it. But we got through no problem. This time. I wouldn't look forward to this every time; they'll definitely think I'm up to something when they clock me every few weeks. Probably think I'm sort of hubba-bubba mule.

As we walked through the airport you couldn't help but be impressed. I'd read that Singapore airport didn't mess about but blimey. Millions upon millions must have been spent. Cinema, swimming pool, game zones, massages, exhibitions, everything. Apparently the fish in the pond cost £100,000. Of course none of this impressed or excited me as much as when we got through into the arrivals area. There wasn't a cabbie waiting with my name on it, it was Grace. Holding up a big handmade sign saying, *'MY DADDY.'* Not daddy, *my* daddy. How cute is that?!

She saw me and sprinted over. It was a real movie moment, I dropped my bag and ran towards her, half expecting to be rugby tackled by security but I made it and picked her up, swung her round and caught a small Asian man in the head with her feet. Apologies were made and he went off mumbling something. I didn't care, I was hugging my princess. I opened my eyes and there was Syd, smiling and holding three coffees, she was good really you know. Poor Kate struggled over with the cases before I realised and I ran to grab her coffin sized bag. I held Grace in one arm and wheeled the case in the other. Shit. What about my coffee!

"Dad, did you see the fish?" Grace strangely asked first.

"I did pumpkin, I saw they were still looking for Bob too."

"What? Who is Bob?!"

"You never seen that all fish are just swimming round mouthing BOB? BOB?" I did the mouth action of a fish.

Grace laughed. My god, I'd missed that laugh, I'd missed everything. And it had only been a month!

Syd walked us to the car. It was a top of the range Merc. I expected her to get in and drive it and her tell us how bad it is driving here but no, there was a chauffeur. It wasn't even hired, it was their driver and car provided by Lucy's company. She was certainly doing well.

She introduced us to their driver, Brad. That didn't sound very Singaporean, nor did he look it. "He's from Australia," she said, before adding as we climbed in the back, "oh and he's deaf."

"Deaf?" Kate asked. "How does he know where to take you if you change your mind mid journey?"

"He can lip read."

"But his back is to you when he's driving," Kate was genuinely perplexed.

"Oh right, he has a tablet up there on his dash and we communicate through that, you see, there's ours," Syd said pointing to a fancy screen in the back.

"Very clever," Kate admitted. "So there are no issues with reading whilst driving or anything like that?"

"You'll soon see there aren't many laws on these roads! Hence why we don't even bother trying."

"Never mind that," I started. "How do you know he's Australian? I mean, the accent is normally the giveaway."

"Erm, I'm not sure," Syd answered. "I think I was told by the company. They must have seen his passport or something."

"So basically, he's just Australian in his head?" It was probably the strangest statement/question I'd ever said.

We had been in the car about half an hour when we reached their house. And to say I was impressed is an understatement. Singapore full-stop was amazing; no wonder people are itching to work there. The buildings were ridiculous, billions and billions must have been spent creating this modern country. I'd obviously done my research about the place that was stealing my daughter. It was only about fifty years old in theory, the biggest religion was Buddhism and about five million people lived here. Which sounds a lot for a smallish island but when you think how many live in London it's not many at all.

We got out the car and Grace couldn't wait to show me her bedroom. I got whisked past Lucy and I think a couple of maids and taken up to the third floor of this incredible house. If an eight year old girl could design a room this was it. A princess vanity table, a palace-shaped bed with a slide, a walk in fucking wardrobe, en suite and obviously everything pink and white. She didn't have posters on her wall but actual artist drawings of Disney characters and pretty things. I should have been delighted for her and I showed her I was but all I could think about is how fucked I am. I couldn't compete with this.

Still, I wasn't going to let that worry me, I was glad she was happy. I returned back down stairs carrying Grace, who hadn't actually shut up she was so excited. She was filling me on the new Jumanji film, from start to finish. I didn't have the heart to tell her I'd seen it. When we got downstairs Kate was talking to Lucy and Syd, with a cocktail in her hand. Never mind Grace living here, I wanted to move in.

"Singapore Sling," Kate said, tipping her glass my way.

"When in Rome I suppose, where's mine then?"

"Rana, can you pass Tom that other drink please? There you go," said Lucy. It didn't look like her first drink of the day. But hey, it was nearly 6pm so who am I to judge?

"Thanks mate," I said to this bloke. More staff I assumed. "Cheers everyone."

I put Grace down and took a big gulp of this rather nice cocktail. I was still on AM time in theory but I couldn't actually give a shit. I had to adjust right?

"We thought we'd head to SKIRT tonight?" Lucy said, like I knew where she meant.

"Unlike you to fancy a bit of skirt!" Had I gone too early on my first lesbian dig?

"Ha-ha, oh how I've missed your vulgar whit!"

"It's actually one of Singapore's best restaurants," Syd added. "And they treat Grace brilliantly."

"Yeah daddy, last time, they took me in the kitchen so I could do my own ice cream. They showed me how to cornetto it."

"Quenelle darling," corrected Lucy.

What was happening?! "Well I like Cornetto's," I said and winked at Grace. I drained my drink and picked her up. "I'll go wherever this little cherub wants to go. SKIRT, t-shirt, pants, McDonalds wherever."

"Well the table is booked for eight so I'll get Rana to show you the guest suite and you can freshen up and we'll head out." Lucy gave it as an order.

"Sounds great," said Kate.

"I'll show them mummy," Grace jumped in.

"Come on then gorgeous, which wing are we off to?"

"I'll get Rana to bring your cases up if you want to head up now," Syd added and pointed at the cases for Rana's benefit.

We headed up to the room with Grace and it was pretty impressive. I reckon we could actually spend two weeks in this room and not need to leave. They even had an intercom to the kitchen. I was looking forward to getting some time alone with Grace over these two weeks, and Kate. I couldn't leave her with the ladies of the manor. But I knew I'd have to give it a couple of days, one to get my bearings and two, to give Lucy a chance to show off how good they had it here.

We got taken to this restaurant called SKIRT and it was rather spectacular. Harvester it wasn't. I had planned to take them out on our first night and pay but Lucy said this is her treat as she picked the place so I went to town! I had grilled octopus to start, which was about £30, for a starter, oh yes, I was going to get her back for stealing my daughter away across the world, bit by bit, starting with the most expensive things I could find on the menu. My eyes went straight to the bottom of each section of the menu. I didn't even like octopus! I told Kate to go for the Wagyu beef starter but she bottled it and went for, what was basically mushroom soup, although it was called something stupid like funghi porcini. For the main I ordered tomahawk steak, it was well over £100 but I didn't even flinch. Unfortunately neither did Lucy. She simply said, "Good choice, it's exquisite here." What a prick. Kate had charred sweetcorn ravioli. What was she doing?! It was literally next to the lobster on the menu but half the price. I'd have to have words. Amazingly Grace, whose last meal I cooked for her was macaroni cheese, had ordered Wasabi crab donuts. I assumed it was because she saw donut but no, she was into it. She proceeded to tell me how much she loves the food here, not just at SKIRT but Singapore and Asia generally and how she plans to be a chef. Fair play, it might change as she's only eight but I told her I'd share my pie recipes with her one day.

"I think we can aim a bit higher than a few pies don't you sweetie," Lucy jammed in, probably getting me back for ordering the tomahawk steak.

"I love Daddy's pies," Grace simply replied and it brought the biggest smile to my face. Take that you rich, snobby, lesbian, girl-stealing, big-footed bint. (She had size 9 feet; I should have known then that she was into women.)

The rest of the night was pretty decent. The food was brilliant and I worked my way through nearly two bottles of red wine, some wine I'd never heard of but it was near the bottom of the wine list so it was very good. And expensive.

We got back and I took Grace up to bed. We chatted more rather than read a book; I suppose she wouldn't have many books read to her anymore, she was approaching nine so double digits next year. I asked what she wanted to do tomorrow and she told me she wanted to show me around Singapore. How smart was this girl, I knew I was biased but she was amazing.

I went straight to bed from her room, not wanting to chat anymore to Lucy. Kate was already showered and was getting into bed. We had the best sex we'd had in months!

The next morning we were called down for breakfast, a Rana special I assumed. Lucy had gone to work and Syd said she had a lot to sort today so she would leave us to do what we wanted with Grace, or should I say what Grace wanted to do with us and that she'd let Brad know and he'd take us where we wanted to go. I hated that Grace was so far away from me but my god she had it good here.

Well it was the first day and I was knackered by the end of it. I think we pretty much covered all of Singapore. It was a really spectacular place. We'd sorted plans for the rest of the week too. Universal world, swimming, the zoo, sightseeing, a trip to Malaysia. It was going to be a busy week but I was looking forward to it. Whatever Grace wanted to do I was doing it. Except go up to the top of the Guoco Tower, fuck that. I did find it fascinating about how many high-rises there were. I had to google it but there are seventy-two buildings over 150meters high, thirty-two are over 200meters. That's more than Kuala Lumpur, Tokyo and even Chicago. Still, I wasn't going anywhere above the third floor.

We met Brad's wife. Brad obviously couldn't say much but spoke to us through the iPad. He said he needed to drop something back to wife and if it was okay to do it now. Of course it was, I told him and got the feeling Lucy didn't allow things like this. Turns out, unbelievably Brad's wife, Jess, was blind! We went in for a cup of tea to meet her and she was great. But I had some serious questions!

"How did you meet?" I asked with genuine interest.

"We got together back home, Queensland," She said, with a still strong Aussie accent. "We lived in the same block of flats and my mum introduced us when we met him in the lift one day." She continued, "Funniest thing was, I'd obviously heard him and I would often say hello only to be ignored. I thought what a rude bugger. But he smelt so great."

The iPad beeped as Brad was smiling as he had been reading lips.

I read it and smiled, "He says he waved at you each time."

She laughed. "So he says!"

We were getting ready to leave when I asked Jess how they communicate on a regular basis. "We have mobile phones," she said.

"How does he hear what you say on a mobile?"

"We have text messages."

There was a small pause.

"Right, now you know what my next question is going to be don't you!"

Jess laughed and told me how her mobile text messages come out as a talking voice. Even as far as describing an emoji if one is sent. I was impressed and pleased to see these two people, probably both in their 50s, find extreme happiness with each other, despite having these long-standing disabilities and the fact he had to work for Lucy!

Lucy, the destroyer of my world. What killed me more than anything though was how right she had been to bring Grace out here. I'd only been here a day and a half and could already see it really was a great place and Grace will blossom into a wonderful young adult.

Shit.

On the journey back home, home? I mean Lucy's. I was thinking about the possibility of moving here but had to dismiss it almost as quickly. I had Kate, and Connor. I suppose he was a big part of my life now. I had no money, even though I owned my house and the mortgage was relatively small. But I had no transferable skills. And to get a job here would be nearly impossible. I could get Lucy to pull strings and get me in at her place but I'd rather chew glass. She'd probably stitch me up and give me Brad's job anyway. No, England it was for me, but with as many trips out here as I could manage.

The next morning Grace went into school. I went with her (and Brad) to drop her off then asked Brad to just drop me anywhere decent in Singapore, which he did. Kate was still in bed so I thought I'd have a bit of an explore. I was dropped at Raffles and went in for a coffee, bit early for a Singapore sling I thought, as it was about 9.30. I almost convinced myself it was like 2:30am back home so I could in theory allow it. Then I saw it was nearly £50 so stuck with the coffee.

Whilst I drank it, which had to be fairly quickly, it came out, at best warm, now it was bordering cold. Mental note to drink iced coffee from now. It was about 35 degrees each day anyway. But anyway, as I drank I started to hatch a plan, a long term plan, and nothing sinister before you think that. But I was thinking pies. A pie shop over here. Would it work? I could save up for a few years, wait for Connor to turn eighteen, ship him off to the army or something (joke) and move out here and open a British pie shop. My surname was sodding Skye, it even rhymed with pie. Skye's Pies. Oh yes, project pie was on. I just wouldn't tell anyone.

I thought more about it on my walk back. Could it actually be something I could do? My pies were good but do Singapore's finest business bods like pie? There were a lot of ex-pats and other nationalities all over the place but I'd guess, like Lucy, they'd be more into caviar and quail shit. I'd have to do some research. Hell, I had about five years to do it! I just hoped it was a legitimate thought and possibility. Not just pie in the sky. Oooh, another idea for the name of it.

I got back to Lucy's about 10am and Kate was buzzing around the room looking for something as I walked in. She found one of her flip flops under the bed; the other was on her foot.

"There you are you little bugger," she said and turned to me.

"You talking to me or the flip flop?" I smiled back.

"Ha-ha, the flip flop. Why are things always in the last place you look?"

It always came across to me as such a stupid saying that. I mean, you've found what you were looking for so you're not exactly going to carry on looking for it are you? But I kept that to myself

"Grace get into school okay? What you been up to?" she asked.

"Not much." *Except coming up with a cunning life-altering plan to move you to Singapore in a few years, away from your only son, something I've literally just had to go through and absolutely hated.* "Have you had breakfast?"

"Yeah, I had grapefruit, which Rana insisted on spooning out for me."

"What, and feeding you it? Like here comes the aeroplane?!"

"No, not quite. But he wouldn't leave me to it. It would do my head in all the time."

"Well, I doubt we'll ever be in the position." I said. "Although…"

"And in his broken English he was informing me how strict Lucy's diet has to be because of her Irritable Bowel Syndrome and that she's got a gluten issue. I couldn't get away quick enough!"

"Well, I can't say I'm surprised about the IBS. I can't stand her so no wonder her bowel is irritated, it's got to put up with her 24/7!"

"Come on, she's not that bad you know, it's just you being on a downer about her."

Downer was a bit of an understatement I thought; she's pretty much stolen my little princess and made her a perfect life without me. Downer, did not start to cover it. But, nothing was going to knock me off my good mood today so I didn't say anything.

"Yeah maybe. Just let me know if Lucy starts rubbing your leg or something okay?" I was only half joking. "What do you want to do today then?"

"Fancy a bit of Malaysia?" She said with a big smile.

"Yeah. Why the fuck not?! Sure it beats the shit out of Herne Bay."

ELEVEN

We got over to Malaysia. Eventually. My god that was an effort. I looked on google maps and it is literally 5km away from us. But it took two sodding hours. We didn't use Brad and made our way over on a train. But you have to get the train to the Singapore side of the bridge, passport check, on a different train from this area called Woodlands, over the bridge, off the train, passport check, back on the train and into Johor Bahru Central Station. And the queues! I'd never seen anything like it before. Those idiots that queue up in January outside Next in Leicester Square would shy away from these. A fella on the train told us 350,000 a day commute over to work in Singapore from JB. (I was picking up the lingo, JB was Johor Bahru and KL was Kuala Lumpur. That was as much as I'd picked up to be fair.) People live in JB because it is so much cheaper than Singapore, so much cheaper that they will stomach that bridge twice a day. Of course my ears pricked up a bit because I was thinking if JB is much more affordable than Singapore I could perhaps look into that. Especially once we got in a cab and the driver was showing us all the cafés and restaurants that he says people come over from Singapore just to visit. One little shack I'd call it at best, apparently got coach loads coming over every day. It looked like a real armpit too.

We asked the driver to take us to a nice fish restaurant and he didn't disappoint. About fifteen minutes in this cab, or Grab as it was, sort of an Uber deal over here. We were on a bit of decking out over the water, now facing Singapore, eating some lovely fresh fish, which we picked out from a tank ourselves, poor things! The Grab was RM10, which is Malaysian Ringgit, and equates to about £2. This delicious fish was less than £10 for both of us including rice and drinks. Oh yes, I could get on board with Malaysia.

"You seem so much better recently you know," Kate said to me as I spooned my last morsel of fish in my mouth. It was a spoon too, they didn't seem to bother with knives over here, and forks were pretty scarce. Mind you, a lot of people I saw were just fist-balling it into their mouths. Kate said it was their religion. Don't think I could get on with that. I did see one bloke doing it though and he had three fingers fused together on one hand, obviously some sort of birth defect but all I could think was how he was winning now, scooping a shit load in each time with his shovel digit.

"You know what, I feel it," I said wiping my mouth. "I like it here. I like being near Grace, I like being away from the cold."

"Yeah, me too. I'll really enjoy these two weeks."

Should I test the water?

"Could you ever see yourself living out here?" I asked as casually as I could.

"No. I'm very much a home girl, Connor would hate it too." She answered without flinching. Maybe my plan wasn't going to be viable after all but hey, it was a five year plan, I had time to work on it, I mean her.

We took in a bit more of Malaysia, or more like a tiny part of the south of Malaysia. There was a lovely marina called Senibong Cove that we had a mooch around in. Quite a lot of ex-pats were here. We could tell because they actually had pubs in amongst the restaurants. I hadn't seen any in the towns we'd driven through. Well, except for the Irish bar obviously. I reckon there was even one of those on the moon. We'd clocked a LEGOLAND and another zoo which we thought we'd bring Grace over to. And there was a load of Islands off both the East and West coast. I fancied that, a couple of nights on a small exotic island with Kate and Grace. I googled it and thought I'd book us a couple of nights when we got back to Lucy's. I'd have to check with her, of course, which just pissed me off but if I'm honest, I wanted to nick Brad to take us as well.

We got back around 6pm. I had planned to get back to go get Grace but that bloody crossing. Of course she was fine and I told her about my island plan. And I promised I'd pick her up for the rest of the week.

I'd cleared the island plan with Lucy and Syd, I asked if they wanted to come through gritted teeth but I think they understood and declined, so I got it booked. Next week we'd be off to a resort called Bayu Lestari on a little island called Pulau Besar. It was off the east coast and we had to get there from jetty about an hour from the Malaysia side of the crossing. Brad was taking us and would be there to get us two days later. Sorted.

Later that evening I'd taken Grace up to bed. She filled me in on her busy day; it was hard being eight apparently. I lay next to her until she fell asleep, I actually stayed about ten minutes after she'd gone off, just stroking her hair and wishing I could do this every night. I returned downstairs and into the kitchen. It was a Friday night and the cocktails were on the go. Time to try and bury the hatchet with Lucy. Last week I wanted to bury the hatchet in her head but my mood had changed and I needed to grow up and live with the situation.

It was a good evening, Rana, who I assumed lived here as he was always here, was knocking out cocktails and nibbles throughout the night and we all got on well, laughing and chatting and joking.

"So how are your group of mates?" Syd asked me.

"All good thanks. The Bates are still the same, she's the boss still. Stuart's latest girlfriend is rather young."

"Young?!" Kate jumped in. "When he wants a blow job he has to say things like here comes the choo-choo to get her to open her mouth!"

"Kate!" I was shocked. Although I could see she was well cut.

"Okay. She's not like two. But she's not twenty."

"Sounds about right for him," Syd interjected. "What about Paul and Debbie?"

"All good. In fact I forgot to say, she's pregnant."

They both gasped.

"They both know how to do it? I'm shocked," Lucy said. "Blimey, I wonder how the kid will come out, either a real trigger or an absolute genius!"

"Come on now. He told me that Debbie reads a book every night and has done since he met her all those years ago." I said.

"Really?!" All three of them said.

"Yeah honestly. And she's nearly finished it."

We all had a giggle before Kate said she needed to go to bed. I wasn't ready and said I'd take her up but would be back down. I got Kate into bed, undressing her just because I still liked to perve over her a bit and left her to go to sleep, on her side.

I got back downstairs and found Lucy heading up to bed too. I thought she best not head to my room! Syd said she was still up for a few if I was. You see, a couple of weeks ago I'd have made an excuse and gone to bed but I like the idea of this. As I have said a few too many times now, as much as I wanted to dislike her, I couldn't.

There weren't any awkward silences that you might expect. After all, I was actually chatting to the person that stole my, albeit pretty much unwanted, girlfriend. And from her point of view she was chatting to her lover's ex. I would say her last bit of cock but I won't be that crass. Knowing Lucy, maybe I wasn't anyway.

"Yeah I always wanted a better surname really," I was saying mid-strange drunken discussions.

"What's wrong with Skye?" she enquired.

"Well for starters you go through school getting called 'TV'. And it rules out ever marrying a woman called Isla."

"I guess," she sniggered, "but your surname could be like mine, which is awful. But not as bad as my first name."

It dawned on me I don't think I ever knew her real name. "I've never even thought to ask you. I knew Syd was short for some Italian surname but never really knew what, or what your first name is."

"What? My surname isn't Italian, unfortunately. It's Polish. Sidgrowgen. My name is Barbara Sidgrowgen."

I spat my beer out.

"Jesus, stick with Syd and burn your passport! No wonder I didn't know it! Does anyone?!"

"You can take it to your grave!" she demanded.

"At least my grave won't have your name all over it like yours will!" We both laughed. I carried on, "Yeah, it would be so cool to have a surname like a movie star, you know like Pacino. How good is that, Tom Pacino!"

"Yeah or like Syd De Niro," She added.

"Tom Stallone," I said and we both nodded with approval

"Syd Willis," she said next.

"What?!"

"You know, as in Bruce Willis?"

"Oh I knew who you meant but Syd Willis?! You sound like the eighty-two year old captain of the bowls club. Syd bloody Willis." We both laughed, had a couple more drinks and stupid conversations and I went up to bed. I had contemplated telling her my plan but glad I didn't. Nobody needs to know and when someone does, it'll be Kate that needs to hear it first and get on board with it. I put a couple of feelers out there with Syd though. I think she'd help out when it came to it.

TWELVE

The week and the following weekend was good fun. We spent a lot of time letting Grace pick where we were going and she tired us out. So much so, Kate actually got ill on the Sunday evening. *'Something I ate I think'* is what she said, wouldn't have surprised me either, one place we ate on the street I think they cooked the food on their van's engine! She looked in a bad way though and worst of all, tomorrow was our island excursion.

"I'll see how I am in the morning but I won't hold my breath, I feel like boiled shite," she said.

"Shall I shift the booking to just doing Tuesday night instead of Monday and Tuesday?"

"No. I want you to go with Grace. Enjoy your time together just you two. We go home on Thursday."

Don't remind me. "Don't be silly, I want you there too, you'll not get to see her much now."

"Honestly. The idea of a boat right now fills me with dread and what if I get ill on the island? I assume the doctor will live in a hut with shrunken heads around him with smoke coming out of them."

Don't know where the hell she thought we were. "You're the best, you know that right?" I said, so grateful to her. Not because I didn't want her to come, I really did, but I really wanted this getaway too, a chance to put my own stamp on a place out here with Grace. I already asked Syd and Lucy not to ever take her here. Lucy sort of scoffed and said *oh okay, we'll make do with Bali then.* But this summed up Lucy, I assumed she always tried to make it sound like a joke but normally it came out like a cutting jab. But what Kate had offered summed up the lovely Kate. A real star.

Monday morning came around. Up at 6am as Brad wanted to get us to the jetty in plenty of time. Grace had this week off school. Syd simply told the school I was visiting and she wouldn't be in for the week. Imagine that back in England? They'd want to fine you £10,000 and give you the electric chair.

We were packed and had filled our stomachs with some of Rana's weird sweetcorn and peanut-butter pancake things. (They sound terrible but it works.) We were in the car for 7am. The crossing over the bridge, 'the causeway' I found out it was called locally, was actually fairly clear going that way, it was chaos the other way but that wasn't our problem today. It was clear but still took over an hour. How did people do this every day? Mind you, was I thinking about doing it in the future too? I knew I'd never be able to afford Singapore to live.

We made it to the east coast of Malaysia and a place called Mersing Jetti at around 10am. It wasn't that far but there weren't any motorways. In fact, on the way there were signs telling you to watch out for elephants crossing the road! Actual elephants. And we saw quite a few monkeys on the way. It was a fascinating drive.

The boat was coming at 11am so we had a bit of time to kill. We had a slow look around the harbour and got a drink. It wasn't exactly the deserted platform sticking out into the sea I was expecting. It was busy. There were a lot of fisherman trawlers and old boats with plenty of people keeping busy. There were even a lot of tourists with their backpacks and cases which I wasn't expecting. Then a ferry came into port, I was calling it a port now because jetty was a huge understatement. This ferry pretty much cleared everyone with bags and cases. They were off to an island called Tioman. Excellent for diving by all accounts and about two hours away by this ferry. I was told our crossing was twenty minutes.

The ferry departed and Grace and I waved them off; everyone was friendly here. Then a little speed boat docked, not a fancy one, one that looked like it may have been doing this journey since Noah did it in his Ark. But it looked fun.

It was only us two, plus the, what, driver? I couldn't stretch to calling him a captain, he had flip-flops on for starters. Another man at the dock helped us on the boat and untied us and away we went. Bobbing over the sea, fairly quickly but the water was like a duck pond. We saw the ferry that left about ten minutes before us as we raced by it, rather smugly waving at them. About fifteen minutes later we saw the island and were approaching a jetty, now this was a jetty.

We were helped off the boat and said thanks and goodbye to the 'driver' and were greeted by a couple of Malaysian women who welcomed us to their resort. It was like paradise. We walked down the jetty, which looked like teenagers had built it as it jutted out a good fifty-meters I'd say. There were no sides, just blue, clear water on both sides. Two days here? I wanted two years! Grace was so giddy, she was constantly just grinning from ear to ear. At the end of the jetty we started to look down on the beach then onto a path which led us to a reception. It was a reception in a wooden building, again looking like it had withstood a few hurricanes in its time. I think all the staff were there waiting, all six of them. It Looked like a manager, a cleaner, a handyman, these two women that walked us down the jetty, not quite sure why, and a chef.

They pointed at the other side of the hut to a few tables and chairs and told us that was the restaurant and when food was served.

"And is there a bar?" I couldn't help but ask.

They just pointed to the same area. No problem I thought.

"Tomorrow, we do you beach barbeque no?" Said the manager in pretty good English.

"Lovely," I said and looked at Grace who was still smiling away.

"Please follow and we take you to room."

"Okay thanks."

And we were led off down to the beach and were shown into, again, hut is about right. But you're never going to get a hut in a better place. Right next to the beach with a bit of decking over the sand, a palm tree loping over it and the sound of the waves. It was heaven. Even inside was better than expected. A modern bathroom was downstairs off a room with a small sofa, table, kettle and a fridge. The bathroom was actually outside, obviously walled off but no roof, suppose it stops those stinky poo's lingering. Upstairs led to a mezzanine balcony with two single beds. It was lovely.

"Where's the TV?" Grace asked with astonishment.

"No TV sprog. We will just have to chat! But I did bring monopoly."

"I'm the car!" she yelled

She only said that because I would want to be the car. Mind games hey, trying to get into my head. The monopoly games had already begun.

This place also had no Wifi here, the main reception did but it didn't reach the rooms. Which again, I liked. Grace didn't have a phone anyway. Yet!

We unpacked and went for a slow stroll along the beach, just up to our ankles in the sea. We walked up to the restaurant and had lunch, which was very good. Then in the afternoon we were in and out the sea, building sandcastles and rock statues. It was exactly how I pictured it. We were the only ones on the beach. It was a shame Kate wasn't with us though, she'd have loved it too. I would say she will be okay to come next time but maybe I'd keep this just for Grace. And there were about a hundred other islands and resorts so we could pick another when there's more of us.

Later we showered and cleaned ourselves up. (I'd forgotten how annoying sand actually is.) Then we headed out again for something to eat. I noticed a couple of the staff members fishing off the jetty throughout the day so I wasn't surprised to see fish on offer. After a lovely bit of dinner, we hung around in this reception/restaurant/bar/recreation area. They had darts and a pool table, a table football and loads of board games. We had a great time!

At about 9pm Grace was starting to look tired, it had been a long day. I said to her let's go and walk to the end of the jetty, there was a picnic table at the end of it under a little roof. Dark sea is kind of creepy but she agreed. I took my beer with me, and Grace her Capri Sun, and down the jetty we wandered.

It was all lit up and looked gorgeous. We got to the end and sat down. It was absolutely silent except for the sound of the sea. We chatted for about twenty minutes about how she liked it out in Singapore.

"I dooo like it daddy, but it would be better if you were here too."

"I know princess, I wish I could be here too, I miss you every minute of every day."

"Why don't you move here then?"

"I'm afraid it's just not that simple. There's Kate and Connor, our house, my job. Not that I wouldn't be out here in a shot if it was possible, but it just isn't. At least not yet."

"Why don't Kate and Connor just come as well?"

"Well, Connor has his daddy back in England so even if Kate did want to move here we wouldn't be able to because of Connor and his dad."

It went a bit silent as I could see Grace pondering.

"But mummy brought me here and you are in England."

This girl was bright. And not wrong! Yes sweetie, that's because your mum is a heartless slagbag waste of hair.

"You're so smart you know that? I know princess and you make sense, but your mum got this great job and hopefully it'll be a brilliant experience for you. Imagine when you're older telling people you lived in Singapore and could just pop to a tropical island for a day. Actually scrap that, they'll hate you!"

Grace giggled.

"It won't be forever gorgeous. If I tell you a secret do you promise to keep it?"

"Cross my heart," she replied, doing the action. "Can I tell mummy though?"

Best I didn't tell her my plan. Especially as it'll take years. Quick think of a secret.

"This is a special island. It's just for me and you. We'll come here every year and nobody will know what it's like. It'll be our little secret."

Jesus that was lame. And kind of sounded a bit like a creepy uncle. But she bought it and zipped her lips and threw the key into the sea. As she did it, we noticed two female members of staff coming up the jetty. Surely we are allowed up here? It's lit up and there's seating.

"Hi, okay if we sit?" one of them asked.

"It's your island, of course."

We had a little, broken chat but got the jist of what they did and how long they'd worked here and I explained our situation.

"She's a beautiful little girl," one said.

"I'm not little!" Grace moaned

"You don't need to tell me. Luckily, she looks nothing like me!"

"She do. Very much but with long hair."

I normally say, *does that mean you think I'm beautiful then?* But I didn't bother. It never ended in a yes anyway.

"So. You jump in yes?" the other lady said. They did tell me their names but I couldn't understand what they said and couldn't ask them to keep repeating. I just became that stupid Brit abroad didn't I.

"Jump in?! In where, there?!" I said, pointing at the sea. "Sod off!"

"You turkey?"

"Turkey? What does that mean?!"

"Scary cat, no?"

"Oh, chicken?" Grace laughed as I responded. "I'm not scared but I'm also not stupid."

"You should, it's good."

"Go on then, you first." Bearing in mind this woman was covered everywhere but her face.

Up she got, ran to the end and leapt in. What the fuck! Her friend was just laughing. Grace was cracking up too.

"Go on daddy!"

"NOOO!"

"Turkey," Grace said, and smiled sideways at me.

"Okay, I will," I said, "but only if you jump in after me." Grace was a good swimmer but I wasn't sure about this!

Please say no, please say no, please say no.

"Okay," she said.

Right, fuck it, make memories I thought, hoping it wouldn't be my last. I took the money out my pocket and put it under one of my flip-flops, had no phone on me so no problem there, and I took my top off. Grace took her flip-flops off and was ready too. I had my good shorts on and Grace a pretty dress but obviously no swimming costumes were required.

"We'll do it together daddy."

Hang on.

"Should I go first in case of rocks? Or you know, sharks?!"

"No shark. No rock." The woman was climbing back up the steps at the side and looked invigorated.

Fucking hell. There was a long pause as I tried to think of a way out of this.

"Come on then," I said taking Grace's hand.

"One, two…… three!" We both counted and then ran and, "Whhhhoooooaaaaa!" The screaming was definitely louder from me. Sppplashhh.

Quick back to the top, I was still holding Grace's hand as tightly as I possibly could. We broke the water back at the top and burst into laughter. What a buzz! It was probably a good six or seven foot leap and it felt great.

"Again daddy!" Grace said as she started back towards the steps. I wasn't going to argue. I loved it.

The water was warm, dark and deep but not as freaky as I thought. I just tried not to imagine what could be below us. The fun outweighed any concerns and Grace living her best life was by far out-doing absolutely every concern I'd normally have.

We carried on jumping in, climbing out, in, out, ridiculous how much fun it was, for about twenty minutes. It was like one of those arty-farty adverts you get at the cinema, with impossibly good looking people jumping into clear oceans and having their photos taken looking perfect. Advertising some sort of colour in a camera or something stupid. When we had finally had enough, we climbed out. On the table the two women had left a big towel and two mugs of hot chocolate. I loved this place.

It wasn't even close to being cold, despite the hour. There was a very slight breeze and we sat on the seat. I wrapped the towel around both of us. We sat facing out to sea drinking our hot chocolate. We didn't talk too much. I was wishing this could last forever and trying my best not to think about the fact I had to go home in a couple of days.

"I think we should come here all the time," Grace said to me. "I love it and I love you."

I was trying my best not to become a crumbling mess. Or in fact, going up to the manager and asking for a job and just not taking Grace back.

"Don't worry gorgeous girl, we will come here every single time I'm over here. It'll be our place forever. I promise. In fact, I'll book us in when we head back to reception."

"When are you back?"

"I'm all booked in for your birthday already. But I'll get over here before then too. But I'll book it here for your birthday."

"That will be so cool!"

"It just kills me I'll have to go so long without seeing you. You know that, don't you?"

"Yeah."

"Who knows, maybe one day not too far into the future I'll look into getting out here full time."

"That would be so good!" Grace gasped.

So I'd sort of made a loose promise. My pie plan was going to be a real idea. I could do this. We sat for another ten minutes staring out to sea and listening to the waves. It felt like Louis Armstrong was right. We had all the time in the world.

THIRTEEN

The next day we had our barbeque on the beach, which was huge for just the two of us. We ended up getting the staff to sit with us and they were real good fun. Just as well because if they were dull it'd have been a really weird afternoon. We had steaks, burgers, chicken, prawns and fish. And a crazy amount of salads and sides. If it was just me and Grace we'd have been eating for a month.

We both slept afterwards. We woke up and spent the last bit of sun on my new favourite seat at the end of the jetty. No jumping in tonight, we just sat and chatted, mainly Grace chatting about everything that is important to eight year olds. The sun disappeared and we headed back to the reception area. We couldn't fit any more proper food in but we got a few snacks and a couple of drinks and played monopoly. Going to bed that night, as much as I loved it here, my head wouldn't empty the dread that loomed over me. I was flying home the day after tomorrow.

We woke up and got ourselves ready, both quite sombre as we didn't want to leave.

"We'll do longer next time smasher," I told Grace.

"Like a whole month?!" She asked with hope.

I hugged her head and gave it a kiss. "Let's start with a week hey," although a month would suit me fine, but was never going to wash. Ooh, maybe I could say definitely a month and then wait for Lucy to pull the plug and be the baddie?! No, I'm past that now. I hope. I had to keep her sweet because who knew how much help I was going to need with *'operation pie'*. Mind you, I'd earmarked Syd for that.

We had breakfast and went for one last sit down on *our* bench. We sat not saying much and waited for the boat. That in itself was a good watch. We said our goodbyes to the lovely staff and told them we'd see them in December. I'd booked us in provisionally but obviously would have to clear it with Lucy, and Kate actually.

The boat trip back was exactly the same as when we came over, but with no smiles. Grace looked great though. Life jacket that was well and truly strapped tightly and the wind almost blowing her hair off. But as I watched her I knew it would be an image I'd keep for the rest of my life. Such a beauty and as much as it pained me, in line for an amazing life here in Singapore. I couldn't jeopardize it and I knew it now. All I was going to do was plan, albeit long term, to join her out here rather than encourage her to come back to gloomy old England. This was her life now.

We docked back on the mainland and there was good old Brad, he wasn't facing us and like an idiot I shouted his name.

'Daaaaad' I think was Grace's reaction. I was waving as well to be fair, at the back of his head. Just making it sound worse now really.

We got back to Lucy's and had lunch and filled everyone in on our escape. We made a promise not to make too big of a deal about it so nobody wanted to go. Kate looked better than when I left. I hoped that the other two hadn't seduced her whilst I was gone! Paranoia was definitely worse in me these days. I made a couple of quips about it to try and gauge a reaction, but got no responses that gave me reason to worry. Of course I really wanted to ask if she'd been fingered by the blister sisters whilst I was gone but stopped short. I could do with keeping this relationship.

We went out altogether for our last night, my shout, and I let Grace pick where. Told her to aim low of course. I had planned to take just Kate out somewhere nice as we hadn't done that since we got here but I wanted as much *Grace time* as possible. I think Kate understood that, as always. After the meal we headed home and I put Grace to bed. I lay holding her until she finally went to sleep. She'd cried but I held it together. I went to bed straight after, laying down and closing my eyes as the *dread* of what was to come tomorrow swept through my body.

I didn't sleep well that night, as I expected. I wanted to go and wake Grace up and sit downstairs and drink hot chocolate but that wouldn't be fair on her, nor Kate as I'd have been a zombie for the long journey home. When I finally got up around 6:30am, I didn't want to talk to anybody. Kate tried her best to cheer me up, even staying naked in the bedroom as much as possible but not even that was working.

We had to leave for the airport at 9am and we'd decided to say goodbye to Grace here at the house rather than the airport. I'm still not sure whether that makes it easier or not. It's impossible to put into words the feeling you have when you have to leave your daughter. I try and get through it by thinking about how the hell people cope with death. I tried to tell myself I was in fact lucky. I would see her again. It didn't help at that moment. We were hugging goodbye when Syd put on our Luis Armstrong song. What the fuck was she trying to do to me?! I was holding it together until then. I left at the end of the song and she told me about having all the time in the world. How she was still only eight I'll never know. Kate was already in the car in tears. Syd couldn't hide it either, tears streaming down her face. Even Brad was wiping his eyes. Lucy wasn't. I said goodbye to Syd, and then hugged Grace once more. Obviously sticking my finger up at Lucy so Grace couldn't see. She kind of smiled it away but knew I actually meant it.

I told Grace time will fly although I didn't believe it myself, and jumped in the car. Even though I felt more like jumping under it. I didn't speak at all until we got to the airport where I had to thank Brad and gave him a hug. He held me that second longer than normal to let me know he felt my pain and it would be fine. And I hope to tell me in a way that he'll look out for her. Well either that or he had the hots for me.

We got through the rather tedious and rigorous security and sat to wait for our flight in a bar. At least ten times I considered just saying 'fuck it' and staying. But every time I looked at Kate I knew I couldn't. I think she maybe half expected me too. Poor Kate. What a situation to be in. She knew I was never going to be the same again. I tried picking myself up for her sake but I just couldn't. I thought about drinking loads so they wouldn't let me on the plane but then thought I might end up in some Asian jail.

The flight was fine, long, but I managed to get some sleep. Kate just sat and held my hand not saying much. I wondered how long she would put up with me for. Here I was with this gorgeous, kind and intelligent woman and all I could do was sulk.

We got home before midnight as we gained our hours back. I didn't go to bed; I went and got a pad and wrote at the top of the first page:

SKYE'S PIES   - Plan.

FOURTEEN

The next few weeks were horrible. *'Don't worry it'll get better' or 'but what a life she's having'* I was getting told regularly and getting more pissed off every time. I'd still spoken to Grace every day on Skype. For the first week she did it through tears. Was I doing the right thing leaving her there (not that I had much choice)? She started to get back to herself the second week and we slipped into our old routine.

Things hadn't lifted my mood though and Kate was starting to get, not annoyed about it, but the sympathy was wearing thin. And I couldn't blame her. I'd arranged a night with Bates to try and take my mind off things and maybe talk through a few of my plans.

When I got to the pub I'd already had a text from Bates saying Paul was coming too as his Nan had just died. So we said we'd best get Stuart too so he wasn't left out. CK wasn't coming.

"How you holding up my old mate?" Stuart asked Paul once we sat down.

"Not too bad I suppose. I'm just surprised she's gone. I really thought she'd live to be 100."

"Ah. I'm so sorry mate. Were you close?"

"Well she was 94 so I wasn't far off!" At least it made us all laugh.

"And how you holding up?" Paul asked me.

"Who knows mate. Not well I suppose." Was my best response. I wasn't sure what I really expected tonight. I planned to talk through my long term goal. I should be speaking to Kate about it first but I thought I'd better get my ideas out there and if they're laughed off I'll have a better idea about how to approach her.

"It'll be alright mate," Bates said. "You'll be back out there before you know it."

"I know but I miss her so much. She's already nearing nine, how quick has that gone when actually being properly in her life? Imagine if I only see her six or seven weeks a year. She'll be eighteen before you know it. Then where's my role?"

"I know pal. But what can you do?" Stuart said, more of a statement than a question.

"Interesting you say that." I'd brought my research book and told them my plan.

"So, hopefully in the fifth year from now, Grace will be thirteen, fourteen later that year, I'll have saved £20,000. That's only £4,000 a year from now so £85.00 a week. As long as I keep my job and don't spend silly money that's totally doable. And I'll sell my house, which I reckon by then, if the market stays fresh, will have around £250,000 equity in it. I won't need that much to lease a business and the rest is to live comfortably whilst it gets up and running. And all these figures here are based on Singapore prices. I could live a much richer life in Malaysia which is basically yards (but hours) away."

They were looking at my figures in the book, or should I say Bates was. Stuart was heading to the bar and Paul took his phone out, he had other things on his mind to be fair. But this is why I only really needed to meet Bates.

In my book it had costings of premises, home rents, cars, licenses, visas, food costings etc. Everything I could think of and could get a rough idea of through my old friend Google. Bates was nodding along.

"Yeah. I don't see any reason for you not to at least give it a go. My only question is why wait until five years from now? You could put your house on the market tomorrow and you could be there in five months, never mind five years."

"I'd love to. But it's Kate. Or more specifically, Connor. In five years he'll be eighteen."

"What? And you'll be okay to just leave him then? He'll probably still be in school."

"No. Not so we can leave him, but he can have a say about leaving his dad. Which is the last thing I would want to do to anyone but I need to think about myself here. And Grace."

"Well, I suggest you speak to Kate then. ASAP. She might not want to go anyway."

"I guess." I strangely hadn't really given that much thought. "I suppose if I speak to her now it'll give us a chance to talk things through in no rush. I think she, if she does fancy it, will want to wait until Connor is eighteen so he can leave his dad."

"What's that?" Stuart said, sitting back down with our drinks.

"If we go out there it can't be until Connor is eighteen to make his own decision about leaving his dad," I told him.

"Eighteen? Nah mate, it's sixteen," he told us.

"Are you sure?" Bates said.

"Course I'm sure. That bitch ex of mine has been priming Jimmy to do just that next year. Whorebag."

I took out my phone to google it. I couldn't really see anything definitive on there. It'll need more research and help maybe, but sixteen? Maybe my five year plan just became a three year plan.

FIFTEEN

Six months had passed. I still hadn't brought up my plan with Kate. I'm not sure why really. Maybe I didn't want the pain of trying to think of something different if she was a straight out no. And I was enjoying the planning. Excited even.

I'd been back to see Grace twice in this time. Both times alone as Kate had work and didn't want to take Connor out of school. The first time I went back it was great to be back. I only did ten days and spent most of it, as you can imagine, with Grace. I did a fair bit of research though and even looked at a couple of premises.

I went back in December for Grace's ninth birthday. Again it was great. She had a little bash for her birthday with a few friends then I got us away to our island, just for one night. The staff there again were brilliant and even sorted a cake. There were a few more people there this time, still only about ten guests so we let them join in on our celebrations and cake eating. At the end of the night, we were sat on our jetty watching the waves gently wash about. I'd brought a Bluetooth speaker with me and thankfully it worked. We danced our Louis Armstrong number on the end of the jetty. What a time to be alive. It might have looked weird from the shore, but I didn't care. Although I did explain it to them later. And they loved it and one American said, "That is like soooo awesome. It'll stick with me like, forrrevvvarrr." Later we got everyone to the end of the jetty and we were leaping in. It was truly memorable. Again.

Of course the dread of leaving and coming back to England was hanging over me again once we were back on the mainland but it wasn't as bad as before. I was sneaking off to view another shop in the morning and I was buzzing.

The shop was perfect, two and a half or maybe four and half years too early but it's exactly what I had in mind. And affordable. In theory. Of course it all came crashing down when the estate agent asked if I wanted it and I asked if I could think about it.

"Sure. Let me know in the next couple of days. And if it's good news I'll bring the paperwork and do the checks. Just to make sure you're not a criminal!" she said and laughed.

Shit. How the hell had I forgotten about that?! I wasn't going to be able to set up in Singapore was I. I suppose I could get a business in Syd's name or something but I was never getting a visa to live here. How the fuck had I forgotten that? My mood changed drastically. But in the Grab heading back I started googling Malaysia. Maybe, just maybe I could salvage something. I mean seven miles from Grace was definitely better than seven thousand.

So here I was, it was January and I was about to drop it on Kate. I'd done my Malaysia research and I could definitely still do this.

We were watching tele and Connor had gone to bed. I switched it off.

"Can we talk?" I asked. Hopefully not sounding like I was going to dump her.

"Sure," she said, looking a little apprehensive.

"You know I've been struggling since Grace went. And you've been great by the way, but I can't get back to being myself. I'm sure you've noticed?"

She just nodded, wondering where this was going.

"Well, I'd like to talk to you about putting a plan in place, a long term plan, about maybe us moving out there?"

She started laughing.

"What, just up sticks and head out there? Forget our lives here and just move there and what, live with your lesbian ex?!"

"No, obviously not. We could get our own place, easily."

"And do what?! I don't think you'll fancy couriering on a moped out there."

"I'm going to open a pie shop."

Even more laughing. And on hearing it out loud in this circumstance I almost laughed too.

"A pie shop?! In Singapore?! Are you actually a little bit mental?"

"No. Of course not," a long pause. "It'll be in Malaysia."

The smiling had gone from her face and she was shaking her head.

"You know this is crazy right?"

"Why is it? I've been doing plenty of planning and there's nothing stopping us giving it a go."

"Giving it a go? This isn't skateboarding or an escape room. This is our lives. Am I supposed to just phone my parents and say I'm off to Singapore? I'll give Connor a note to take into school tomorrow shall I? I won't even bother telling his dad."

"You're being silly now. I'm talking three or so years down the line."

"It's just not possible. I can't just leave my life here. I don't think you can either."

"Kate, Grace is my life. And she *is* over there".

That hit her quite hard. I don't think she was shocked by it, she always knew how I felt but maybe she thought I was doing this with or without her. Unfortunately, she was right.

I slept in Grace's room that night to give her plenty of space and thinking time. I didn't know how the morning was going to go. I got up and headed out to get a takeaway Starbucks for us both. It'd give a chance for Connor's dad to get him and leave us alone for this Saturday morning. Plus a Starbucks might remind her of how we met.

I went in and she was sat at the table and I sheepishly said hello.

"Hi," was her reply. She continued, "You didn't have to sleep in Grace's room you know?"

"I know, just wanted to give you some breathing space." Plus I didn't mind sleeping in there if I was honest.

"Well I certainly did some breathing. Deep breathing to start with to contain my anger. Not anger actually, I wasn't angry, I think it was shock."

"Look, I didn't want to just spring it on you. But I've done lots of planning and thought it was time I talked to you about it."

"I just don't think I can Tom. It's just not me. And then there's Connor. I don't even know where to start with that."

"I'm not saying, *come on, let's do this and book a flight*. I'm talking years down the line, Connor will be older and we can make real plans."

"So you just want Connor out of the way?!"

"Not at all, I'm thinking more about him being old enough to decide for himself. It takes the issue of his dad out the way."

"And do to him what has just happened to you."

I saw that coming.

"I know, I know. But I can't keep going like this. I just can't. It kills me a little bit more every day I don't see her."

"But it'll get better. It'll get easier."

"Will it? Do you know that?! And do you know what? I don't want it to get better. I want to be near her."

There was a long pause.

"I get it Tom, I really do. But I just don't think I can do it. You do what you have to do but I just can't."

She got up to walk away and as she passed me I grabbed her hand.

"Look. I don't want to do this without you. And I really want to do this. Just promise me you'll have a look at my ideas and you'll think about it? We can even go out there and get a real feel for the place?"

Silence. I passed her the coffee.

"Come on, do it for Adolf."

At least she smiled.

"I'll have a think but don't hold your breath. I feel a firm no at the moment."

"Hey, that's fine. If you get to a 5% maybe, then I'll be happy."

She left to go get ready. We were shopping soon. This was going to be weird. If she says no then where does that leave us? Do I keep on at her for two years until she breaks or do we just go our separate ways straight away? I suppose the latter would be most likely as we'd be running into a dead end. I couldn't imagine a long distance thing working. If it didn't work in American college movies, it wouldn't work in real life.

The next couple of months were pretty weird. Kate had looked at my plans and agreed to come over next time we went, which was at Easter in a few weeks. I thought, or more likely hoped, she was warming to the idea. We both agreed to not say a word of it to Connor. Or anyone else at all actually. I still hadn't mentioned it to Syd and Lucy.

The trip out there was, as usual, brilliant. Grace, approaching double figures later in the year, was looking taller and older. And was certainly wiser. Far too clever for me. She wanted to play scrabble constantly and I got told not to let her win. Pah, as if I would. But I couldn't bloody win.

Grace had a couple of days still at school so Kate and I nicked Brad and got over to Malaysia. After plenty of scoping we found a place called Danga Bay. This was the place I knew was *the* place. It would be perfect. Ten minutes from this side of the causeway after crossing from Singapore. It was modern, vibrant, exciting. And plenty of international people mixed in with locals. Plenty of professionals and blaggers. The whole place was less than five years old and it was kind of like a mini city in itself. Lots of apartment blocks overlooking the sea, lots of nice hotels, shops, restaurants, pools, a cinema, bowling alley and all sorts. Apparently people came on holiday here and lots of people lived here. People even travelled here just to try this stall that sold *Pisang Goreng* or in our terms, simply fried banana. And although I didn't think I'd travel far just for a bit of battered banana, once I'd tried it, I agreed I probably would travel across Malaysia for a bit! It was gorgeous. But of course what was more gorgeous was the fact people were travelling here because of a stall that sold bananas basically. All I could think about was *'wait until you've tried my pies!'* I'd been to quite a lot of towns over here now and only one place I'd found sold pies. It was at a place called Forest City. It was a similar place to Danga Bay but further from Singapore. It had a golf course and a duty free shop so that's why most people came here. I knew it wouldn't be for the pie that I tried. Tasted like an out-of-the-packet from a services job. Yet the staff told me customers couldn't get enough of it. Maybe pies out here wasn't such a crazy plan after all. I enjoyed the rest of the travelling and looking around and doing a bit of, I guess, light consumer research (it made what I was doing sound better and useful).

And the best news of all. Kate liked the place too.

WHO'S FOR PIE?!

SIXTEEN

Kate came back out to Singapore with me in August when we flew out for just a week. She was definitely on board with the Malaysia pie plan now. She said it was a scary thought but you only live once. And I suppose she wanted to make me happy. We viewed a few places and moved on a bit more with our plans. Grace, I still didn't say anything to. I was perhaps going to just not tell her, come out here and take her to our place as a surprise. Could I pull that off? Hopefully. But we did have to talk to Syd and Lucy about it. Not that I needed their blessing but obviously it's something that needed to be discussed. Those two didn't bother me though, it was Connor. And his dad.

We'd decided we'd stick with my original plan. Move out there at the start of the year after next. So roughly eighteen months time. Connor would turn sixteen in January. Again we decided not to tell him until the January coming up after Grace's tenth birthday. He'd have a whole year to process it, we'd sort schools or colleges and get his dad on board. Simple right?

It was agreed I'd go back to Singapore in December for Grace's birthday, take her to our island and at some point speak to Lucy and Grace about our plans. I couldn't wait. For any of it. I wanted to talk to anyone and everyone about it but couldn't. I could talk to my mates about it so had arranged an evening at ours for everyone and their other halves and had them coming round for, well, pie. Paul and Debbie would bring their baby, Harper. I still wasn't sure if that meant it was a boy or a girl.

The evening was going well, the pie was savagely devoured by all. I'd made eight different types of pie and made them in decent sized dishes so people could tuck into whichever they liked best, or as I requested, try them all first and then go for their favourites. I made a couple of simple ones, chicken and ham, minted lamb, steak and ale and a meat and potato. Then I made four newbies, a Coq au vin one, a cheesy steak and mushroom one, which went first although I wasn't that keen, a broccoli and spinach one, which was the last to be eaten, no surprise there and I tried a sausage and mash pie, which was a weird idea but worked bloody well, I thought it was the best one. I'd used four different types from my butcher so every mouthful was maybe a little different. And of course the wine was flowing. Debbie had put Harper, their *daughter,* to bed in a Moses basket in the living room and had put the monitors on. I was kind of glad because it meant everyone stopped swooning and I could talk about our plans!

I kind of regretted it as it was getting scrutinised by everyone.

"But what about Connor's dad?" It was Yvonne's turn to twist the screw.

"Well, it's a tricky situation. But at the end of the day, we have to do what's best for all of us," Kate answered.

"But how do you know this is the best thing?" Yvonne continued.

"We don't. But we think it could be. Why live wanting? If it doesn't work out we can just come back," Kate said. I was unsure if I was reading her tone correctly.

"You're about to do to his dad what Tom has been torn in half about!"

"Not exactly," I chipped in. "I mean, if it was avoidable it would be great but it's not. And Grace was taken from me at eight years old. I'd brought her up and saw her every single day. Connor will be sixteen, his dad sees him once, sometimes twice a week."

"But that doesn't mean he deserves this."

"I agree but what do you want us to do about it? Ask if he wants to come with us?!"

"Well, Syd asked you if you wanted to?" Paul's turn.

"I know but *that's* different too. It's just not the same." I didn't really have conviction in my answers but I couldn't explain it.

"What has Connor said?" Bates asked.

"We haven't spoken to him yet," Kate answered sheepishly.

There was a bit of silence.

"Well," Bates broke the silence, "I'm sure it'll work out whichever way it works out. But I'm just not sure how ethical it is."

"Ethics?" I raised my voice a bit more than I intended. "Don't talk to me about ethics. Where have ethics got me so far? I'm seven thousand miles away from where I want, actually, where I need to be. If I have to upset a part time dad to get what I want then hey, I'll do it!"

More silence, drooped heads, dessert being poked around plates and wine glass swirling. Until Stuart finally spoke.

"Ethics? Isn't that what Chris Eubank calls the county just above Kent?"

Thank god for that. It was shit but it made us laugh and we all lightened up a bit.

"If it helps mate," Bates said, "I think it's, in fact we all think it's a great idea, brave but exciting. We just worry about the Connor situation. But it'll work out and we're all here to help."

"And you bring a whole new meaning to the *'chef's special'* sign don't you," Yvonne added somewhat wittily.

"Also, your pies are literally the best thing in the world," Debbie said.

"Yeah, they're fucking great," Stuart eloquently stated. "And I can think of worse places for me to visit on holiday three or four times a year!"

"Three or four hey? Dream on," Kate said with a smirk. "Anyway, enough about this, how's it going with hatchet Hannah?" He'd started seeing a girl, unbelievably, from the abattoir.

"Yeah, that's over that is. It hadn't been going well so I thought I'd surprise her at work but she didn't like that. She came to where I was waiting after finally getting somebody to go and get her (they're not the brightest at that place). When she finally came out she was covered in blood. *Sorry, had a squirter*' she simply said. Anyway that put me off her instantly, but she's dynamite between the sheets so I thought I'd let it go. But she didn't look in the mood for the ham and tomato sandwiches I'd brought for us. She told me to go and not to bother her anymore. She said she needed her space but I think there was something else going on. I hung around and I heard her say something and I could hear everyone laughing, you know, over the bleating. So I didn't mind it being over to be honest. She smelt of offal all the time anyway."

"She was *offal* to you then?" Paul said in a terrible Scottish accent.

"I'm not ready to joke about it though," Stuart replied.

"Oh be quiet. You've never taken longer than a week to get over a girl," Yvonne quipped.

"He's never taken longer than a shower!" Bates added.

"Hey. I'm like an onion I'll have you know," Stuart said. I think he was being serious but I'm not sure.

"Why an onion"? Debbie asked. "Because you cry a lot?"

"No Debbie, onions believe it or not, don't cry. They have layers, like me," Stuart sarcastically replied.

"Oh. Okay, I'd never heard that before."

There was a bit of silence and I got up to go get more wine.

"So you could say you're like a cake?" Debbie continued.

"What?" Stuart said exhaling.

"You know, cakes have layers too. And they're much nicer than onions."

"Okay, thanks Debbie, I'm a Victoria sponge, okay?"

Debbie smiled and looked genuinely pleased to have come up with it.

"You could say Eskimo then," Paul said out of the silence.

"Jesus Christ!" Stuart belted out. "Cos' an Eskimo has to wear layers in the cold yes? How about just fucking off?"

The rest of the night was fairly sensible but also quite drunken. Paul stayed sensible as he was on baby duty and they left first at around midnight. The Bates had their sitter until two so left just before but Stuart stayed. He wanted to tell me what a great idea it was that I was going and he'll support me all the way. He was pretty drunk but I knew he meant it. He even said he might do it with me but I was hoping he'd forget that!

I ran a few name ideas past him to see how he reacted. Kate had gone to bed so basically I was just killing time with him waiting for him to go. He had it in him to drink through until 6am easily so I was hoping to bore him with these names.

"Skye's Pies, makes most sense," I'd started, "but it doesn't make too much sense to people that don't know me."

"Unless you open one up at the airport," he added.

"Good point. Pie Oh My, Graceful Pies, Full of Grace pies, Pie'd off, Pie south of Thai..." Everyone I came out with didn't sound like what I wanted. I went to get some more wine and as I came back in Stuart was asleep. I guess I had bored him enough. I put a blanket on him and went to bed. I did worry about him, he wasn't in his best place at the moment. I think he fully expected to be well and truly settled down with a couple of kids, an estate car and mowing his lawn every Sunday. But he just couldn't keep it in his pants.

December came round and off I went to see Grace. It was great as normal and I saw her turn ten. Double digits. We didn't make it to our island but we said we'll go at Easter. I got my dance with her at her party but while doing it, I wondered how many more I'd get. I thought she started to look a bit embarrassed in front of her mates and I understood that. But I thought it's only about two minutes a year so she'd have to suck it up! I spoke to Syd about it and she said that even if she does it through gritted teeth for a couple of years, by the time she's sixteen or seventeen, she'll love it again.

I think I agreed with her and decided to bring up about moving out here and the pie shop. She thought it was a great idea. And offered to help me anyway she could. I said maybe she could keep an eye out for premises for me. She said she'd love to as she's a bit bored so was grateful for something to do. *Get a job,* I thought, but kept it to myself. She told me not to tell Lucy yet, I'm not sure why but couldn't think of a reason to disagree with her. I also asked her not to say anything to Grace as I wanted to keep it from her so I could do the ultimate surprise.

I was back in England before Christmas. Saying goodbye to Grace never got any easier but the light at the end of the tunnel helped me through it massively. I still couldn't help thinking about how much of her life I was missing out on.

Christmas and New Year went well and it was January 6th and we sat Connor down to tell him our plans. Kate was extremely nervous about it and we had spoiled him over Christmas to try and soften him up a bit I guess. I didn't realise how much was riding on this conversation until I looked back on it. I just assumed he'd say yes and the big problem would be the dad. I was very wrong.

"NO WAY!" he yelled for about the seventh time after we'd told him.

"Don't you want to come out there at Easter and have a look at least?" His mum calmly asked.

"I'm not going, ever, you can't make me. Why do you want to go, just to stay with this loser?"

Bit harsh I thought, we'd never been completely at ease with each other, fair enough, but that was out of order. I'd been in his life for a long time. I went to pull him up but Kate put her hand on my leg to keep me from saying anything.

This carried on for about fifteen more minutes until he finally stormed off. His parting shot was, "I'll just go live with dad, he loves me more anyway!" Sorted I thought.

But no. Kate was in tears and I couldn't say I was surprised, the way the brat erupted.

"What are we going to do Tom?"

Let him live with his dad and we'll go, was my preferred reply but now wasn't the time.

"It's okay, let him calm down a bit and we'll speak to him again. Maybe even with his dad?"

We sat in silence for a few minutes when we heard the stomping down the stairs.

"I've googled it, you can't make me go. I'll be sixteen so you can go, and kiss my arse!"

"Right!" I was up and heading towards the little twat. "We will then. I'm going to sort it for next week so we go and stay there. See how you get on without your mum shall we. See how quickly you get fed up with McDonalds with your dad. Or more likely until *he* realises he can't send *you* back." It was harsh but I wasn't having him being rude.

"Tom!" Kate yelled. "Go to the pub, leave us to talk this through."

"It's eleven in the morning," I said.

"Go to Wetherspoon's then!"

I wasn't going to argue, I wanted out of there. I wasn't going to bloody Wetherspoon's this time of the morning though. I went to the café and ordered the fattest breakfast I could see.

I was there for over an hour, I had four sodding cups of tea but the breakfast was a cracker. It was the last thing I was going to enjoy today as I got a text from Kate at about 12:30 saying:

COME HOME. WE NEED TO TALK.

Everything was about to go to shit.

SEVENTEEN

Kate was in bits when I got home that afternoon. She said she simply couldn't do it without Connor coming. I was gutted but I completely got it and expected it. There was no way she would come without him and I'd always known that, I just thought the little twerp would jump at the idea. I was wrong.

We spoke all afternoon about what to do. I obviously wanted to still go in January, that still gave us a year to work on him and get plans in place. Kate said there will be no way he'll change his mind and had gone to his dads now to tell him all about it. I felt for Kate, I really did. It was an awful position and situation. It was also one I knew I couldn't win. But I wasn't ready to give up on Kate yet.

"Look, let's not make any rash decisions. Let's take a couple of months and reassess," I sullenly suggested.

"I just don't think anything will change," Kate said, and it was followed by silence until Kate raised her head from her hands and said, "How about we just put our plans onto a longer scale and go when Connor is eighteen? He'll maybe be more up for it then and we could get him into a Malaysian or Singaporean University?"

I didn't want to bring her down as she almost looked excited again but. "But what about if he still doesn't want to. Would you still want to? Or will you then say let's wait until he's twenty-one? Don't forget, the reason for this is to be near Grace. I'd rather do that before she's got grey hair."

More crying. I took that answer as no.

"Can we just plan for three years? Please? I will be ready by then and we could really work at him."

This is exactly what I didn't want. I wanted to go yesterday, certainly next January, I didn't want to wait three years. "Let's not talk about it anymore hey. Let's have a few days." It's the best I could do.

"Okay, it'll be your choice though. It's three years or nothing from me," Kate said, and got up and walked out the room and into the bathroom.

Fucksake. Bollocks. I loved Kate and didn't want to lose her but could I put this back longer? I thought back to my original plan and it *was* five years so maybe I could. But I didn't want to. Could I do this? Fucking hell. What a shit day. This had gone horribly wrong and I was thoroughly pissed off. Things couldn't get any worse. The doorbell went.

I opened it to Connor's dad. More specifically Connor's dad's fist. I didn't have chance to react and was on my hallway floor with blood streaming out of my nose before I knew it and the doorway empty. The fuckwit had gone.

I couldn't blame him of course. I'd have probably wanted to do exactly the same thing if the roles were reversed. Which I suppose they kind of were a little while back. Not that I know what the punching equivalent is when it's a lesbian. Steal their batteries I guess.

Later that night Kate and I had a good chat. My nose was throbbing but at least I was getting sympathy from her. We decided not to make any decisions any time soon. Which I hated. But what could I do? I fully understood the situation and hated seeing her so torn by this. Well, not torn, I knew which side of the tearing she was on but it didn't make it any easier for her.

My relationship with Connor had completely gone. Probably getting drips of nonsense from his Neanderthal father. But my problems with Connor inevitably rubbed off on Kate. Six months down the line we agreed to put our plans back. We'd now be making the move in the January, after Grace turned thirteen the month before. Connor would be eighteen. I wasn't happy and it showed. I was still doing my trips out to see Grace, the only thing I found myself living for. I didn't like my job, Connor had made sure I wasn't enjoying my home life anymore. I understood he didn't want to come but why he kept digging me out and snarling at me when he wasn't ignoring me I didn't know. Can you steal a mum from an eighteen year old if you're also invited along? But worst of all was the breakdown of mine and Kate's relationship.

She said to me how different I was in the two weeks before I went out to see Grace compared to the two weeks after I was back. Even though she had always noticed this, it was the fact the two weeks after became the same as the whole time, until the two weeks before. So basically all the time. I knew it too but couldn't do anything about it. I'd said I'd put it on hold so didn't know what else to do.

My first trip to see Grace, I told Syd what had happened and the plans were on hold. She genuinely looked disappointed but got the deal. The rest of the trip as always was brilliant. I didn't go to Malaysia again that year except for going to our island. Which was the opposite way in Malaysia to Danga Bay where I planned to set up sticks. I was tempted all three times I went that year to just stay there but couldn't do it. Not to Kate.

After Grace's birthday that year, her eleventh, I thought, two more years, this year had flown so will the next two right? But Grace had changed so much over this year I didn't know if I could last it out. She wasn't *as* excited that I was there this time, she had her eleven going on twenty-one hub of friends and if they weren't physically with her they were constantly on the end of her phone, either facebooking, tweeting, texting, whatsapping or actually speaking. Facetime, skype, or old fashioned hearing. I didn't want her to have a phone so soon but what say did I have these days so far away? Lucy's argument had been that she'd have become a social pariah at school if she didn't get one. Bit dramatic.

If I was being completely honest with myself, this wasn't just about Grace any more. Obviously she was 95% the reason I wanted to come out here but now I wanted it for me too. I was excited about setting up a business here, doing something I loved doing and making a fresh start with my life. I was turning thirty-seven this year and wanted to get it going before I was a clapped out forty-year old.

It was on my return that year that Kate and I had to have another discussion. I waited until Christmas was out of the way and waited for her to ask me what was going on. I was so shit at starting these types of things. Once she asked I told her my feelings and said I couldn't last two more years. There were lots of tears but an understanding that this was inevitable. Our lives had been growing apart over the last year and we both knew it. Obviously I didn't come outright and tell Kate it was over. I said I was definitely going at the earliest chance I could and could she reconsider. She told me there was no way she would ever leave Connor, which I totally understood. So in a way, we dumped each other. I did say to her if she really wanted to make the move herself I would wait until she was ready. But I could see it in her eyes, and think I always knew, she was making the move for me and not because she wanted to.

The relief on both of us showed. The sadness and wallowing around the house, the angry answers, the lack of conversations and the lack of sex was all behind us. Yep, we even had some really good break-up nookie, a couple of times in fact. One of the times I even put a little extra effort in just so Connor could hear. The little burk. *Hear that you little shitehawk? This is what your mum will be missing!* Petty but fuck it. Hopefully he'd pass it on to his dad. But this all meant we could both start looking to the future, it was just a shame it wasn't going to be together. We agreed that in any other circumstances we'd be made for life. Another thing I'll blame Lucy for.

Now that Kate and I were sorted, I thought I could start really planning and was extremely excited. Of course, things are never that simple.

EIGHTEEN

The housing market had crashed. Of course it had. Houses just weren't selling. So my main funding was gone. I had nearly £20,000 saved but wanted to sell my house to really push through my new life. I was hoping for at least £200,000 cleared but that had gone. I planned to give Kate a portion of it, I didn't think she'd push me for any but it would have been the right thing to do. I had discussed it with her and we'd definitely have sorted it out.

The estate agents I had round basically said if I wanted to shift it, I'd literally have to halve my estimated value. That, although I'd have cleared some decent money, didn't sit well with my practical mind. Why potentially throw away so much money? And that's when Kate came up with a solution.

"How about I just rent it from you?" she asked over a cup of tea one day. This was mid-March now, we still lived together, got on great as well. A cloud had definitely been lifted with our decision; it was like we both wanted what we wanted but didn't want to tell the other.

"What? As in long term?" I queried.

"Yeah why not? It'll save me having to find a deposit, upfront monthly rent, references, admin fee etc. Plus I'm sure we could come up with the right price. Especially if you needed to come back here for a week or whatever. You could stay here."

"That'd be fine until you have a boyfriend!"

"Well, the offer is there, what do you reckon?"

"Makes sense to me. It'll give me chance to get the ball rolling on getting out there and also the effort of advertising it. But how much you thinking per month?"

We agreed on an amount and sealed it with a shag. This was a weird situation. But hey, I wasn't complaining. I did say I'd move out though to make it at least seem right to take money off her. We set a date of first of June. I would move into Stuart's, he didn't know this yet. As I'd literally only have my clothes as Kate wanted most stuff left, the rest could go to the tip if none of the boys wanted anything. Obviously, Grace's stuff I put in the loft. Didn't think I'd ever need things like a pink princess bed again but I couldn't bring myself to tip it, or any of her stuff.

I moved out on the first day of June as planned. Stuart was not only fine with me staying at his, he seemed positively delighted. "It'll give me a chance to run something by you my old chum," he said when I first mentioned it.

God knows what he had planned. I was sure I would be finding out pretty soon though. Leaving my house, although being slightly sad, I could only see it as exciting. Kate told me the spring in my step recently was actually visible. Her riding me like a bucking bronco helped with that I guess. But mainly, it was months, not years away until I moved nearer to Grace.

Funding was an issue of course, because of me not selling the house, but that was sorted, to an extent, on my trip to see Grace at Easter. And the answer came from an unlikely ally. Syd.

"So I can't sell my house but I should be able to take a loan against it or remortgage easy enough," I was saying, about an hour into our conversation. I spent a lot of time talking to Syd when I was over there. Lucy was normally busy, and I didn't actually want to speak to her anyway really. And once Grace was in bed I suppose it was obvious we'd talk more. But it was never awkward.

"How about a partner?" she enquired, completely unexpectedly.

"What do you mean, you?" I had actually thought how hard this would be, not just financially but physically. It was a two person job really, or an awful lot for one.

"Yeah," she leant forward to look at me like she meant it.

"But can you even cook? I'm not having you throw Rana at me."

"Ah, no. I can't cook, even slightly, but I meant more of a silent partner. Just adding a bit of money to get you started."

"I see," I said and was secretly punching the air. I didn't need much more to get it up and running. I had £20,000. I didn't want to borrow any but this seemed a good option.

"How much were you thinking?" I asked.

"How much were *you* thinking?" she countered.

"We'll it's a bit of a shock to be fair. You could put in whatever you wanted and it'd just determine my premises really. I've got the money to get the required permits and licenses. It's now just down to where and how much it is."

"I've looked all through your plans and ideas and figures and it actually makes sense to me business wise, not just because of who you are. I reckon if I put in another £20,000, we are 50/50 partners."

A small bit of quietness. I wasn't sure about this.

"We'd obviously get a contract drawn up and all the legality of it," she continued.

"The thing is," I started,"I don't want to do this 50/50. I'd basically do all the work AND pay half the money. That doesn't seem quite right but thanks for the offer."

"I see. I get what you're saying but I'd be putting money in and having no say in what is done or doesn't get done. I couldn't stop it going down the pan if you're not up to it. It's kind of how business works mate."

More silence.

"I'll tell you what, let me think about it and tomorrow I'll have a look into how much gets me what and get some real figures sorted. That okay?"

"Course it is. Just let me know. I want to help but I also need to think about this money. It's mine and all I've got. Nothing to do with Lucy you see. So if you could also keep any of my involvement quiet I'd appreciate it. Not just now, but always."

"My lips are sealed," and we cheersed our beers and I went to bed that night with a lot to think about.

As it turned out I wouldn't need that much. But my plan had also gone from a shop to a catering van. Not a shitty one you see at fairs and that, but a converted Winnebago. I loved it. It had all the mod-cons and looked great. It couldn't be driven anymore but to tow it to where I wanted was about eight quid. It was fully loaded. Cookers, gas, fridges, freezers, electric, sink with running water. Perfect, and I could buy it, get the permits to park it up right in the centre of the pedestrian area of Danga Bay, the middle of everything, stock it, plug it into all the main facilities which were already on site at a tiny cost and all for less than £30,000. Syd got on board (the idea not the van). She would add £10,000. I asked if she wanted it paying back a certain amount a month but she said she wanted in, full stop. She would take a percentage every week and that was that. I needed it and she wanted it. It was working out. I even factored in a place to live. Danga Bay had some nice, if not huge, accommodation, again ridiculously priced compared to home. I'd have sea views, five minutes from work and ten minutes from the causeway.

Everything was in place. Deposits and fees had been paid. Visa's and licenses all signed and good to go. Now I just had to wait. And stop my stupid huge grin every time I face-timed Grace.

I was leaving England in December. It was already November and I was starting to get anxious as much as excited but I was told to expect it. My plan was to fly to Singapore for Grace's twelfth birthday. Do the birthday bits and take her to the island, head back to say our goodbyes, see you next year blah blah. But Brad had said he'd happily take us to Danga Bay, 'or home', I would say, eek. And from there fill Grace in. Obviously expecting tears and screams of sheer joy. If she was still my little girl of course.

I'd been at Stuart's for my remaining time in England and I'd almost forgotten to add that he was coming too! I was glad. I couldn't do this alone, I mean the actual workload; I'd need help and it would save me trying to find it out there. Plus it would be a blast.

I asked him what about his job, his son, his life but he simply said, "Fuck it, fuck it all. Time to add some Asian notches to a bamboo bed." Hmm, maybe it wasn't the best idea. But he was in now and that was that. He was going to meet us in Malaysia in January though.

My last night in England, at least for the foreseeable future, was upon me. Bates had invited me and a few friends round for a decent send off. The night was good. Yvonne told me she'd already booked flights for Easter (I thought she was joking until I saw Bates' face). Not that he didn't want to get out there but I guess he thought I'd probably want until the summer to settle in. But that was Yvonne, and who knew, maybe I'd need a little pick up around then. All evening I was happy, thinking about the exciting journey ahead, not what I was leaving behind and who. That's when I finally got caught alone with Kate, which I'd been trying to avoid. I knew I had to do it but also knew it was going to be awful. We'd spent a lot of time talking in groups all night but we'd kept finding each other looking at one another. It used to happen when we first got together but that was to slip off to the bathroom or somewhere, naughtiness in her eyes, this time it was just sadness. And I'm sure mine were the same.

We were in the kitchen when everyone else was in the other room. It was short but intense.

"So," I started feebly.

"Yep, so," simple reply, shit, back in my court.

Silence.

"I don't know what to say. Thanks?" We both giggled. "I only got through the last few years because of you, I hope you know that?" I told her.

"I do. And same for me too. I wasn't in the best of places either you know. You sorted me out."

"Well, what can I say? When you get picked up in Starbucks you must be doing something right!"

"Erm, you picked me up actually," she said with a playful hit.

"No chance! I would never have been brave enough to approach someone like you."

"That's wrong. But nice to hear! So I'm the prettiest girlfriend ever then?" again she said it coyly, with those gorgeous sultry eyes, looking up towards me.

"By a million miles. All the others were right dogs!" She laughed and hit me again and I pulled her in for a long, tight hug. "I'm going to miss you you know, I wish this was going to be different." Thought I'd get it out there.

"Me too. But I'll come and visit, or is that weird?"

"You'd better!" I kissed the top of her head and held her for as long as I thought I could get away with. Partly because I didn't want to let go but mainly I thought I'd start getting a hard-on.

"It's not too late you know," I said. I thought I should even though I knew it was.

"I know. I wish. But I can't." She turned her head the other way on my chest so she was facing everyone in the other room and Stuart stood in an open fridge squirting squirty cream in his mouth and washing it down with a swig of beer.

"Anyway. You've got a new wife to take with you now." We both looked at him. And laughed.

NINETEEN

Grace's birthday was good. She was definitely an early teenager. At one point she asked me why I hadn't stopped smiling?

"Just happy to be with you," I said.

I think the two friends that were flanking her at the time, all with phones in their hands, rolled their eyes at me and said something like '*sooo lame*'. Fuckers, I'd have words about them to Grace when we went away. And to Lucy too. This new attitude needed sorting out before it took control. 'Lame'. I'll show those two prissy pricks lame when I let Stuart loose on their mums. I would say me but that just wouldn't happen. Also, they're twelve, I needed to chill out a bit.

"Dad," Grace came up to me later on.

"Yes my nearly teenage princess."

"God. That's like a whole year away."

"I wouldn't count on it."

"What does that mean?"

"Nothing. What's up?" I patted my lap but got an evil.

"Wellllll, do you know our dance?" Here we go, the beginning of the end. "Is it okay if we do it when we go away? It's just, like, not really something my friends think is cool."

I looked at her. Not hurt by the fact she wanted to hide our dance away but the fact she cared so much about what those two bellends thought. But then again, I'd never been a twelve year old girl I suppose.

"Grace listen," I started and pushed a bit of her hair behind her ear. "You can't worry about what people think about you and things you do or don't do. You are a beautiful, intelligent young lady, you need to be your own person." She looked a little upset. *'You've never been a twelve year old girl,'* I told myself again. "But, yes, I will not get you up to dance if you do not want me to. As long as you promise we do it at some point?"

"I will." She hugged me. Not too embarrassed to do that yet.

"You also need to promise me that you will not do things you don't want to just to please a couple of morons."

"Like you and Uncle Stuart and Uncle Norm," she said, pulling away and giggling. Cheeky little monkey.

"You think you're so smart you," I went to tickle her and she laughed like mad as I did it. It was like going back in time, somewhere in there was still my little girl.

"Daddddd!" between the giggles.

"Okay, remember though. That dance embarrasses me far more than it does you!"

She was running back to her friends when she turned. "With your moves I'm sure it does!" She poked her tongue out and ran off laughing, like a kid should.

The dance I got back at Lucy's house. She said she still loved doing it but to tell me that *'I need to understand some stuff'*. Which clearly I did. The next day we left for the island. Grace asked if Tia and Maria could come. I didn't think I'd ever sworn in front of her before and certainly not to her but this was ridiculously close to it. *'Fuck right off'* I think flashed across my mind first but instead, I calmly explained how it was our island and we should keep it that way. She got that and never asked again, or sulked. Also Tia and Maria, seriously? They were twins but somebody was having a laugh surely. Or maybe just loved that drink. If I did that Grace would be called Tizer. It also turned out that they were fourteen, two years older than Grace. They were in the same school year as it was a small international school. But I didn't like my daughter hanging around with fourteen year olds.

I brought it up whilst we were sat on our bench at the end of the jetty, a place we agreed would never hold any judgements or arguments and she told me that they were the most popular girls at school, and the richest too. I corrected her and said their parents were, not them. I agreed to lay off as long as she used her brain a lot and never did anything she didn't want to; two years was a big difference at this age. I could see why she liked to be seen with them, just as long as they weren't taking the piss. I was pleased I was going to be a lot nearer from now to keep an eye on the wannabe Olsen's.

After our couple of days of bliss we were met by Brad as normal and off we went. After an hour or so we passed the turning for the causeway and Grace clocked it.

"He's missed the turning."

"Has he? I'm sure he knows what he's doing. Perhaps he knows a short-cut."

"Across the water?! Not even Brad is that good!" she said, puzzled.

"Okay, listen, I've got a surprise for you. I'm taking you somewhere before we take you home. Don't worry, your mum knows."

"Is it Legoland?"

"No. Aren't you too *old* for Legoland now?" I mocked. "It's only ten minutes away so you'll soon see."

We pulled up in Danga Bay. Brad dropped us outside Starbucks and said he'd meet us here again in an hour.

"So, what do you think?" I asked, flaying my arms out.

"What? A Starbucks? Brilliant Dad, but there's three between home and school."

"Yes my little smarty-pants, I've asked Brad to drop us for coffee. What about the building behind it? Come on, this way." We walked past the coffee house and past a big silver, closed, Winnebago, and into a reception.

"What's going on dad?!"

"I'm showing you your surprise."

The lift stopped on floor fifteen and out we went. Up to apartment 5 and I opened it up.

"Well?" I asked as we walked in.

"Where are we? What is this?"

"Do you want to see your room?"

"What are you going on about? My room? Are you kidnapping me?!"

Can you kidnap your own daughter? I guess you can. "It's my new home, *our* new home. Well, details of your staying to be determined mind."

"Why don't you just stay at ours when you come over, why come here?"

"I'm not going back. I'm here all the time."

Silence, I assume whilst it sank in.

"Oh my word!" She ran over to me and gave me a big hug. "Are you serious?"

"Nope, it's a big joke, haha. I've just broken in here for a laugh. YES I'm serious!"

"This is the best news ever!"

"What?! Even better than when Mia and Tiara invited you to their palace?!"

She thumped my leg and walked towards the balcony. "It's Tia and Maria silly but yes, I'll let you have this one."

"Awfully good of you fine lady," I said in a mocked posh voice. "Let's show you the view."

I opened the curtains and the sliding doors and we stepped out. It was a bit high for me but the view was brilliant and Grace loved it.

"That's the beach!"

"Oh myyyy godddd so it is. Wait until you see the pools." I had to deflect from the beach, the beach you can sit on and sunbathe but you can't swim in the water. I still wasn't sure why but I'm sure I'd find out. But there were four pools we could use including one on the beach.

"And which is my room?!"

I took her to her room, it was the second biggest one out of three. I hadn't broken the news to Stuart yet but he was last in so it was tough. Plus Syd had been over here for the last month or so getting it ready and setting up Grace's stuff in that room and had done a great job. Grace loved it. Still pink but grown up too. A normal bed with pink covers and pillows, a wardrobe and draws, a little area with a table in it with a mirror and, I guess, a potential makeup area. And also at the bottom of the room under the window a nice desk with some books lined up next to it and on it, a surprise to me, and Apple laptop. There was a note on it saying, *'Enjoy having your dad back, love Mummy and Syd'*. Bastards. That was very nice. But also stealing a bit of my thunder. Bastards.

Syd had done a great job, I don't know who the posters were of on the wall but she seemed chuffed. It already looked like it had been her bedroom for ages.

"I'll leave you here just while I check the fridge is on, I'll need to get food."

Food *and a* fridge by the looks of it. There was supposed to be one. I'll message the landlord later, I am a day ahead of officially being in I suppose. The kitchen was off the lounge which had a sofa and a chair and to the side by the balcony doors was a small dining table and four chairs, which I thought we'd probably use on the balcony most of the time. As I said, it wasn't the biggest of places. I checked my bedroom and if there was an opposite to Grace's room, this was it. There was a bed and that was it.

Yep, definitely need to get a few bits this weekend. Unbelievably, there was an Ikea fifteen minutes away. I'd see if Brad fancied a few extra quid and help me out. Stuart's room didn't even have a bed. I'd best get him one but the rest of the stuff he could get. I needed plates and pans, glasses, cups, kettles, knives, forks, microwave, the whole lot. I had a hob but no oven and hopefully a fridge on the way. Luckily I planned to do a lot of cooking in the van, there wasn't much room in this small, along one wall, 'kitchen'.

"Daaaad!" It was a noise I'd never tire of, I was thinking as I was walking towards her room.

"Yes?"

"What are you going to be doing here then?"

"Come on, I'll buy you lunch."

"And tell me all about it?"

"I'll show you all about it."

We left our new apartment and it was the happiest I'd been for a very long time. Grace took the yellow card to operate the lift (a security feature but you'd be screwed if you lost the card; gets you in the building and to your specific floor).

We walked back out across into the square, thirty seconds from the beach and thirty seconds from the shops and as we walked towards the 'Winnie' I decided I'd call it, we stopped and I pointed at it.

"Here we go," I said.

"You're camping here too?"

The kid is a joke a minute. "Kind of. I'll be spending a lot of time here though. Making pies!"

I opened up the door and in we went. It was pristine, old and well worn but really clean and sparkling where it should be.

"Seriously?! This is so cool!"

That's right, your dad is super cool I was thinking. But this did feel really cool to me too. As you went in the door, you could open up two adjoining side panels that you served through which had a metal work top under it on our side and a fold down one for the outside. Behind you as you faced outwards were three clear ovens, sort of like the ones that hold the bread in Subway. There were two more metal worktops on either side of them. Up towards the other end there was a six burner gas hob and opposite that, a grill. Then up the top was a big fridge and a single chest freezer. And also a sink. As I said, well equipped. Back near the door were a couple of storage cupboards.

"I want to work with you!" Grace said. "I still want to be a chef you know."

"We'll maybe we'll be running these all over the world in ten year's time?"

"That would be lush!" I think her mum had bigger ideas for her but it was nice to hear.

"So, I was thinking we put tables out here," I said as we walked back out and locked up. "We get the use of all this." And there was a decent space out the front. Probably sit between twenty and thirty people easily. There were two more empty bays next to ours and my plan eventually would be to have a bar-van in one and a dessert one on the other side. Then just a big seating area, music and a really good vibe. But I was getting ahead of myself.

"Let's eat. You can help me think of a name."

TWENTY

All the fun was done and it was time for business. Stuart had arrived and we'd both settled in pretty well. Our apartment was looking homely, Grace was staying as much as possible at the moment as it was all new, and I loved that. We did the beach every day and she helped get the apartment right and start sorting Winnie. I'd explained how I thought things would work with Stuart whilst Grace was busy filling our storage spaces with the food packaging we'd be serving our pies in. I'd sorted with a local business to make us these cardboard dishes, we were going full on takeaway vibe even for the seating area so we didn't have to worry about washing up, for now at least. These dishes were probably about the size of a book, had a firm bottom and sides. The idea was to put a rectangular shortcrust pie base in one, then the filling, then a slice of puff pastry sits on top but at a slight angle. I'd tried it a few times over the last week and this was the easiest way to do things fresh, quick and looking good. The three ovens, that were actually a potential six, would be at different temperatures. They were three in a row but you could split the temperature as the lower ovens were actually different, so we had six when needed, which was good because of the difference in pastry. They were big ovens, as in they were high with a lot of levels. I tested and could easily get 100 bases and 100 tops in each one. Five shelves in each, taking twenty on each shelf. Oven one would be where they are put in to start so it'll be fairly high to get the majority of the pastry cooked. Oven two we'd put them in to finish off browning then oven three will be to keep them warm. Hopefully, not sitting in there too long. We bought four, school canteen-like, deep pots for making the fillings. They were separate to the oven and stove as they plugged in and we placed them to the right of where we would serve from. Right next to the worktop that I'd be doing the pastry on, I'd make lots of pastry sheets and put them in the fridge, layers upon layers of them with greaseproof paper in between each layer. But I'd always need space to make some when required. It would also be where I'd be making it every morning. I'd cook the fillings on the stove in batches and keep putting them in the big ones. We'd stick to four fillings a day, didn't want to over complicate it, three meat options and a vegetarian would be the plan. We'd even make and freeze some vegan pastry if it was ever needed. The plan was, Stuart would stay to the left as we looked out and serve the customers, taking the money and giving me the order. I'd do it and he'd serve it out, all depending how busy it was. The idea was to keep it as simple as possible but also that we could cover each other's areas when needed. Not that I'd let him near the actual making of the food, but he knew how I wanted it dished out. We'd bought a fryer for doing fried potatoes (not chips), and we had a couple of deep pans that would sit on the hobs with different sauces or gravy's that would complement whatever we had made. It seemed simple. Hard work and lots of preparation but certainly, with a bit of organisation, the system would work.

We were banding names about as we were getting ready for the launch, hopefully for next week, but were waiting on one last licence, one to serve pork or pork products. Unsurprisingly, hard to obtain in a country with a fair few muslims.

"If they don't want pork, just don't order it," Stuart said.

"It's not about not having the pork, it can't be in the same kitchen," I responded.

"Fucking crazy if you ask me. What's the problem with a bit of pig anyway? Bacon is literally the best food out there."

"I think it's because they think it's a dirty animal."

"What? These pricks walk around with no shoes on, use a hose to wipe their arses after they've squatted over a hole and eat with their hands, but pigs are dirty?!"

"You're going to get on great here mate," was all I could respond with.

"Just fuck em' off I reckon. Tell them they just can't have your pies."

Thankfully Grace walked back in. "So, you got the name sorted yet? The sign needs to be ordered tomorrow at the latest. You're already running late really," she started, before even a hello.

"I don't know!" It was actually doing my head in. "I'd like Pies from the Skye's."

"Ready for when I join the business when I'm sixteen right dad?"

"Yeah that's right pumpkin. Except, if you want to be a chef I think we can aim a bit higher than this don't you think?"

"You sound like mum."

"What about Pie Pie?" Stuart asked. "Sounds like it could be a town from down the road."

"Why would we want that though?" Good point Grace.

"Okay. Piece of Pie?" Stuart came back with.

"But that makes it sound easy," Grace countered.

"Easy to buy and eat, yes. That's my point."

"I just don't like it," I said.

"What about Van-Pie-ers," Grace said.

"That's very clever," I told her "It's just better to say than to read."

"Yeah and it's not hallowe'en mongo," Stuart said and grabbed her and rubbed her head.

"Get off!" Grace said, fighting him away. "It's better than *pie pie*." She returned in a piss-taking voice.

A bit of silence as we carried on doing what we were doing.

"I don't bloody know then mate," Stuart started up again. "Prize Pies? Danga Pies, Pies in disguise?"

"What are they disguised as?" I asked.

"Alright smart-arse. The Pie's the Limit?"

"Sounds limited."

"Ooh, how about we get your beer truck up and running next door and call ourselves..." he stood up and cleared his throat, moved his arms in a grand gesture, "Pioneers of Pie and Beers?!"

I think Grace put her head in her hands around about the same time as me. The door opened and it was Syd.

"Hey up, I've got this for you," she said but I'd turned the other way so didn't know she meant me not Grace.

"Hey, Pie guy! Here it's for you," as she threw me a package. Never mind the package, Grace looked at me and then I saw Stuart looking at me too, both smiling and nodding. She'd cracked it.

"The Pie Guy," I mouthed. "I love it."

"Me too!" both Stuart and Grace chirped in.

"What, what did I do?" Syd asked.

Stuart grabbed her face and planted a big kiss on her lips, much to Syd's distress.

"You magical minge-eating hunk of estrogen!" he said as he pulled away and walked towards the door.

"Good god!" Syd said wiping her mouth. "Please don't ever do that again, god knows where your mouth has been!"

"Probably on a lot less pink canoes than yours Vulverine," and with that he was out the door.

"I hate that man," she said, looking at me but trying to hide a smirk.

I was happy though. We had our name. I still liked Pie's from the Skye's but would perhaps look into that in the far away future if Grace ever got involved with it. I'd have loved that but definitely hoped she'd end up slightly better than someone selling pies from a van, but let's see what I can make of it. I had big plans and ambitions. Of course, it was all in hope as much as anything but why not. We were good to go. Watch out Malaysia and Singapore. It's the *PIE GUY*. Okay, maybe that needed a bit of work.

Unfortunately the delay in the final licence was a long one. We were good to go, as in the van was ready, seating had been bought and so had gazeebos for above them, all the cartons and plastic cutlery were ready. We just wanted an okay so we could go get the food needed and get cooking. It took nearly nine months.

TWENTY ONE

Even though I was frustrated about the delay, it gave us plenty of time to market the place with fliers, posters, adverts and for Grace to put things out on social media; oh yeah, she was a self-proclaimed media manager. But she did a good job and enjoyed being a part of it. But equally as importantly, it gave me nine months to spend a lot of time with Grace. We had lots and lots of fun and good times. She even told me it was the best time she'd had since she moved out here. We got back out to our island again and told the staff about what was happening and promised them free pies when they visited. Brad, and to be fair, Lucy and Syd, had been brilliant. They let Brad loose just to bring Grace over after school a couple of times a week and for the weekends. I'd head over to her for a couple of days too, Brad even came and got me. I liked Brad, the fact he didn't speak didn't affect his humour. He wrote on the IPad to me one trip over whilst we were sat in traffic that his wife read horror books. Obviously I bit and asked how? In Braille was the simple and obvious answer. *Why horror?* was my next question, I'd never been a fan, too scary I told him. *'Yeah, but it doesn't scare her, she can feel it when something scary is going to happen'.* That was Brad, a good guy.

The Bates had been over and enjoyed themselves. I think Bates even fancied staying and running the potential bar I had planned. Obviously I couldn't even get my *Pie Guy* off the ground but I was thinking big. Money, luckily, wasn't much of an issue as everything was so cheap out here. But I'd used a fair chunk on reserving two sites on either side of mine. I'd paid a holding fee that would last twenty-four months, at which point I'd have to start paying the monthly fees or relinquish the sites. Not a bad deal really.

Stuart had spent most of his time working his way through the locals. It was unbelievable. They couldn't get enough of him. *"What can I say, I've still got it,"* he tried telling me once, but I think it was more because he was tall and blonde. So basically very different to 99% of the men on offer.

"What they don't have in tits, they make up with in flexibility," he bragged with a wink to me one morning.

"Flexible? As in they can do any night of the week?" I joked.

"Nope, very bendy. One from the other night actually tucked her heels right behind her head."

"Okay," I said, eating my granola. "Sounds lovely."

"It was! It was like fucking a ball."

"Why would you want to fuck a ball?"

It went quiet for a bit whilst he seemed to contemplate my fairly decent point.

"Whatever, anyway, I'm just saying, there's a lot out there. You should look into it?!"

We'd made the agreement that he wasn't allowed women round here when Grace stayed, thankfully. Some of the noises from the room would scar her for life.

"Who was the girl I saw you with yesterday? She looked like she wouldn't leave you alone. I didn't come over in case she clawed my eyes out for disturbing you. It looked like you were trying to swallow her head," I enquired.

"What? That head? It's massive!"

"It was pretty big to be fair, but do you think that's because she was so small?"

"Nope, it's just a big head. 'Snipers dream' I've saved her on my phone as."

"How nice Romeo. I don't know why you bother when you don't even particularly fancy them."

"Got to get my rocks off sunbeam," he said, standing up to take his bowl to the kitchen. "I do occasionally have to sort of fold one in because it doesn't quite go hard enough."

This bloke was a serious piece of work! I think he'd actually got worse over time. But he was always entertaining.

I hadn't actually even thought about sex since I'd been here. I was so busy with either sorting the business or spending time with Grace. And when I did have a bit of time, I still missed Kate. He was right though, eventually I was going to have to do something. But fucking a ball wasn't top of my wish list.

We were coming towards the end of October and finally we got the okay. This was it. November the first would be our launch date.

Saturday 1ˢᵗ November was here. I was nervous. I'd made all my pastry and my four fillings. I'd opted for some classics to start off with. The four options were up on the board, and also a permanent sentence: *fillings will change daily, so come again tomorrow!* Today we had a creamy chicken and mushroom pie, with an offer of more creamed sauce, a slow roasted lamb and carrot pie, with a minted mushy pea sauce side option, a peppered beef pie, with a curried gravy option if wanted and the vegetarian option which was pumpkin and spinach, with a five bean inspired sauce. I'd made lots of the fillings, what wasn't sold would be frozen. I didn't want this to happen as time went on but there was no way of knowing just how busy we would be. I'd made two hundred shortcrust pastry bottoms and two hundred puff tops. With more pastry in the fridge just in case.

Times to open was a tricky one. We'd opted to open at midday until midnight. With us both having an hours break plus whatever other time we thought we could grab. Twelve hour shifts were just the norm out here. People obviously ate lunch, but the people here ate from 9am until 4am, so we would just see where we were in a couple of months. I could make fillings when it's quiet so there won't actually be any wasted time for me in the van. Of course if it was crazy busy, I'd have to work in the mornings doing it all. I think we maybe would like to do 4pm until 2am eventually and get the other two units up and running. *Baby-steps though,* I had to keep telling myself.

So the launch didn't go brilliantly. It wasn't terrible but not exactly rushed off our feet. Just about everyone we served said how nice it was, so that side was good, but we didn't sell a hundred pies. On the Sunday we got Syd and Grace out there giving out samples and getting them pointing our way. Even Lucy came over to help out. Whether she was telling people to go to get noodles instead, who knew?! Sunday was a bit better, over a hundred pies and again lots of compliments. And Stuart pulled so he was happy. As long as he wasn't giving her pies for free I didn't mind what he got up to.

Monday was really quiet, as expected, but the day was ghostly. Picked up in the evening including seven or eight people I recognised from the weekend, so people were coming back, which was excellent. I was mixing the types of pie all the time; we had sausage and onion, curry, pork and leek, beef, lamb, chicken, pulled pork, I actually had a list of one hundred and forty two different pies that had all been tweaked by me, so I had plenty to be getting on with. Grace, who spent all of her Saturdays and Sundays with us, was doing her bits (very helpful), and she actually said I should put on the board, *There's one hundred and forty-two different pies here!* I told her to go for it so she wrote it in big letters for us. The first customer came up and asked me to go through the pies, so I went through the four pies I had that day and he said he wanted to know the hundred and forty-two! I told him he'd have to keep coming back to try them! In fairness, I saw him, Poh, a lot of times and actually we became friends.

We closed Wednesdays (Grace only did school in the mornings on a Wednesday, so Brad would have her at the Singapore side of the border by about 12:15 meaning she'd be with me around 1-1:30pm). We'd planned when (or if) we got busier and needed another pair of hands, I'd take Tuesdays off and Stuart would take Thursdays so we would both have two days in a row each week. But that was maybe just a pipe dream the way things were going!

Things stayed the same way for the first year really. We were doing between one hundred and two hundred pies per day (on a busy day), which was decent but not enough. Not over twelve hours. Lucy was actually helping and telling everyone in Singapore that she spoke to and told them about this 'wonderful' pie van called the *Pie Guy* and we got a lot of people that fancied the trek over.

Of course I was happy just to be near Grace. She'd be over here every Saturday and Sunday helping in any way she could, normally out in front of the van getting people to come and try the food, not that I was pimping her out to exploit her cuteness. But people listened and would come and try it. To be fair though, she would speak to people in English but also clock just what Nationality people were and would speak the bits she could in Malay, Mandarin and Singaporean. She was even learning Japanese! This was one smart cookie.

She'd also be over, as I said, on a Wednesday afternoon and evening with me and quite often would stay until the Thursday, and yep, good old Brad would come and get her at around 7am and she was okay to start school at 9am. That was really good of him, that causeway was an absolute shitter most of the time. I'd actually walked it over the bridge about a month or so ago, much easier and quicker!

I'd managed a night on the island with Grace just before both her birthdays I'd been here for. We still loved it and nothing changed just because I saw her more often. We'd actually grown as close as ever and I loved it. That bratty teenager I thought she'd be, she hadn't become. Not yet anyway. Even on her actual birthdays, she came and asked me for our dance. The one that had recently passed, her fourteenth, we held the party at the van, her choice, and with our speaker system all up and running we actually danced in front of a big circle of observers, *probably* the most embarrassed I've been but it was great. We even made the local online paper! As these Asians loved their cameras, there were plenty of photos going on, and videos, and we became a little bit of a story for a while, which as cringy it made me feel, it helped the business.

We started getting a lot busier, amazing what a little bit of a happy story does to people. They wanted to meet me and Grace, and eat our pies. We got interviewed by a radio station and newspapers and things were starting to fly. About time!

We managed to stay busy all the time pretty much after that, especially weekends. We got the bar on its way to being set up, Syd wanted to run it apparently, but so did Stuart. As it was at that time with the pies, I needed Stuart, and probably Syd too. But it would take a couple of months to get the bar ready so I got Syd to some and help us with the van and then her and Stuart could do a rota for each other for the bar and the pie van. Grace was going to be fifteen later this year so her work load at school was getting heavier and so she often only made it over on a Saturday or a Sunday. I was missing her, and she was missing me, and the van I think. But with work getting busier it obviously meant I was. We planned to open the bar in February and then open both from 4pm to 2am, so it'd give me more time to prepare in the mornings. As it was, I was in the van at 8am ready for the noon opening. Sometimes I was only getting into bed gone 3am and it was taking its toll. I thought it was where I wanted to be, not crazy busy and far from dead. But it was about to get absolutely crazy.

TWENTY TWO

It was later in the summer, around August. The bar was up and running, mainly by Syd although we hired a lady called Ming to help.

"Far from Minging though," Stuart said. "You can tell why Syd hired *her*. Wonder if she is a lip-licker too. Be a bloody waste that."

I told him that there were millions of women in Malaysia and Singapore, don't upset our only actually member of staff.

Anyway, it was around 6pm and things were ticking over. I was in the pie van chatting to Stuart, Syd and Ming were doing the bar. It was a Saturday so all the seats were full and the music was playing and people were generally having a good time and people were constantly coming and going through the day. Some staying and basically eating pie and drinking all day. They can live the dream here you see!

A very attractive, tall Singaporean woman, probably in her early twenties, came up and ordered a pie. It was a ham hock, sausage and cider pie, extremely popular amongst the non-Muslim customers, out of my one hundred and forty pies. Although I would occasionally use all my pies to keep my advert of having so many, I pretty much shuffled about fifty of the most popular over a month. If I was honest, three of the daily pies would be regular appearance-makers, never two days in a row but maybe one would perhaps show up twice a week or a fortnight. This wasn't laziness, it was purely down to sales and customer reviews.

Anyway this woman ordered, got it and off she went. I only really remember her because Stuart was drooling. "Maybe fifteen years ago," I said.

"Even then she'd have to be blind," Syd chipped in as she was walking past our hatch to go collect glasses.

"I'll go find out then shall I?" he said, starting to take his apron off. We didn't wear a uniform but had matching smart black aprons.

"Don't you dare" I said and nodded at the people lining up for a pie. Luckily, for her, we had a queue of nine or ten people so he couldn't get away.

It was about twenty-five minutes later that the attractive lady came back. "You see," Stuart said. "She's coming back to ask me out."

"I don't doubt it stud," I said and leant out of the hatch to see her coming up to us.

"Hi," She said.

"Hi," I returned as Stuart set up a posing stance and said, "Sup?" Classy.

"That food was amazing."

"Thanks very much, we try," was my standard reply in these situations.

"All I'll say now though is, tomorrow, make more pies *Pie Guy*," and with that she walked off, with a walk you kind of had to watch. Stuart looked at me and I looked at him, both with a lost look.

"Jesus," Stuart said to me. "Alright fatty. What was that about then?"

"Not a clue mate," as we both watched her disappear around the corner.

Ten minutes after that, Ming came running over. "Quick, look at this," she said, passing me her phone. I was looking at Twitter. I knew nothing about Twitter.

"Show it to Grace, she's here tomorrow," I said, trying to pass it back.

"Just look will you," she said, thrusting my arm back.

I looked down at the picture and here was this woman, the gorgeous one that had recently left, eating a bit of pie, in the background was our van with the glowing *PIE GUY* sign, with my head poking out of it, the edge of the bar next door and everyone enjoying themselves on the tables. The caption said, **GET YOURSELVES TO PIE GUY ASAP, DANGA BAY. BEST FOOD EVA,** then a couple of hashtags #pieguyrocks and #pieguygreatpie.

"Nice one," I said giving the phone back. "Can't beat a good review."

"Good review?" Ming said. "You don't know who that was, do you?"

"Not a clue."

"That's Adela, she's like *the* biggest star in Singapore and the rest of Asia. She has nearly twenty million followers. Look she's put it on Insta and Facebook too, look."

"Let me see that," Stuart said, grabbing the phone. "Where am I?! Why's it your stupid face showing?!"

"Great, hopefully she'll sing a song about us," I didn't get what this could actually mean. "Maybe a cover of that song from Bad Boys, instead of Shy Guy, Pie Guy?"

"Seriously though mate," Stuart started. "She is massive, I recognise her now. She is like, the Beyonce of the East!"

"Well, she doesn't look like she eats many pies to be fair so I doubt she'll be back."

It was about an hour after that when Grace phoned me all excited.

"DAD, DAD!" she started, hardly breathing.

"Calm down Grace, breath, what's the matter, are you okay?"

"Yep, DAD." A couple of deep breaths. "I'm Great." Another breath. "Listen to me." Deep breath again. " YOU'RE TRENDING!!"

I didn't know what to say, what could I say? I didn't have a fucking clue what trending meant. Turns out it means lots of people are talking about you on the various media outlets. I still wasn't sure quite how that made a difference to me but I was about to find out.

The next morning I'd taken everyone's advice and made a lot of pastry and a lot of fillings. I'd made twenty different fillings, each filling probably doing about one hundred-fifty pies, there'd still only be four on the go but we could in theory do five lots of four, not that I expected to get anywhere near needing it but I could freeze them and use them for the week. I didn't like doing it but thought I might have to soon anyway just to free up more time. Anyway, I couldn't have been more wrong, we could have done with thirty fillings.

As we were prepping from about midday, we could see people starting to mill about, a lot more than the normal ambling crowd at this time. Had a couple of people ask when we were opening. 4pm was the reply every time. Until around about the fiftieth person asked and there were over two hundred people out there! It was 2:30 so we brought it forward to 3pm, which Stuart shouted out. People just started forming an orderly queue. This was mental.

We weren't going to have enough hands. We had me and Stuart, Grace was here ready to do what she could but we borrowed Syd from the bar and got Ming to get a couple of friends in to help her at the bar, which was also crazy busy. Grace *even* got Lucy over and she even got involved.

Grace, who still wasn't quite sixteen at this point, but fifteen going on fifty, was on pie making duty with me. Stuart and Lucy served and Syd took charge of the potatoes and sauces. If you'd told me five years ago about this possible scenario I'd have laughed my head off.

We opened at 3pm and we didn't stop until 2am and that's no exaggeration. I say we, Grace got taken back by Brad at around 10pm and Lucy went too, after all, they had school and work the next day. At around 6pm we were struggling to cope and Stuart clocked a young lad just hanging around and grabbed him to see if he wanted to work. Chad (stupid name), was sixteen and Australian and jumped at the chance. He told us he lived here with his dad who worked in Singapore and was normally bored. He came on and helped all of us when needed. I noticed Grace took a shine to him and he was a good looking lad, tall and tanned. I don't suppose I could have blamed her but I kept her at my end of the van and left him up the other end as much as possible. *Not on my watch sunshine,* is all I thought. Mind you, she was nearing that age now, boys and beer. I couldn't think about that!

The day was crazy and we got through all 3000 pies, somehow. I don't know how many potatoes we got through but we sent Brad three times for big sacks of them. Luckily they didn't have to be peeled! We didn't deep fry them as we started, we just part boiled them then a quick shallow fry with a bit of chilli and spice, crisped up and flavoursome but it did mean a constant need to be on them. Lucy was helping today but we thought we'd get good ol' Chad on this duty if it was going to stay this busy, it would be too tough for Stuart now.

Chad stayed through to the end. He'd messaged his dad and his dad came to see him once he was back from work and we cleared up that it was okay for him to stay out late. It was no problem apparently.

After we closed the shutters that day, we collapsed into chairs out the front.

"That. Was. Mental," Stuart said.

"I can't feel about 85% of my body," I returned as I leaned back as far as I could.

"Here you go," Ming brought over a couple of beers with Syd and sat down. Her two friends left around midnight but were going to work every weekend from now, either in the bar or if Syd wanted to do the bar, she'd send one my way. Chad, stupid name n'all, sat down too.

"Yo Chad Pitt," Stuart darted at him. "Good work cobber, can you have one of these?"

"Thanks but I'd best not," Chad replied, turning down a beer. Good lad but rubbish Aussie, I thought.

"What's your school plan then Chad, what you doing here?"

"I did my exams early so have a year off before starting at Singapore uni next year. I'm just a little bored, my dad works every day."

"Well, if you fancy this every day you're on," I suggested. We needed a potato guy even if it went quiet again. I expected it to go quieter obviously but thought it wouldn't be dead again for months, maybe years. We hadn't had one single complaint today and lots of compliments.

I had to get to bed. I needed to be up again to make lots more pies. Tough one to judge, it was going to be a Monday but would it still be crazy?

Yes it was.

TWENTY THREE

Things never really got back to normal. We were clearing between 1000 and 2500 pies every single day. We still closed Wednesdays but we couldn't get any other time off. It was like rush hour every hour. Chad, stupid name, picked it up quickly; he was a smart lad. The way I was catching Grace having a little flirt with him, he needed to get much smarter though. I'd make a pie out of him. *Aussie Pie.* Which oddly enough gave me an idea for a filling. Kangaroo and lager. I must remember to give it a go at some point. If I ever got the chance.

We were making the main news in Singapore and local Malaysian television, what a success we were and how nice it is. Every time, we got even busier. I still hadn't got around to opening up the other side of us yet but didn't think there was simply enough room for people out the front. It'd have to wait.

I got away for one night that following 12 months, for Grace's sixteenth. We got to the island. I'd have made more of it if I'd known it was going to be my last chance for a long time. We had got so busy, chaotic really and I was struggling. I was knackered. It was a phenomenal success and I should have been proud, or thankful, especially to a random superstar stunner, but I'd lost sight of why I was here in the first place. Grace.

Things got so busy over the following two years I'd started to lose her. After her sweet sixteenth, a special birthday for any young lady, I'd started to only find time for the business. Whenever Grace was due over I'd make excuses as I was either busy sorting bloody pies or if she was round I'd fob her off with watching a film and I'd fall asleep. I didn't have the energy to make our time together as great as I'd wanted. So I could sleep or just relax, I'd even give her money so she could go to the cinema with Chad. Stupid name. I think she understood to be fair but it didn't mean she liked it and neither did I. But it was when I missed her show in Singapore that the wheels really came off.

There was a huge concert at Singapore's theatre and Grace was due a violin solo. Oh yeah, she played the violin as well as speaking four languages and knowing how to make my pies. I knew about it for months, she was so excited and nervous and let me know several times how she'd booked me the front seat right in the centre. But I missed it. I don't even have a good reason that I missed it. I just went home and fell asleep, but it was after a bottle of wine. How could I do this to her?

I woke up to over twenty texts from her and her mum and Syd as well.

WHERE ARE YOU? XX

DAD?

DAD, IT STARTS IN 10. WHERE ARE YOU??

They'd stopped from her after that one and they'd started from Lucy and Syd and they weren't holding back. But the last one from Lucy was the worst. I could take abuse from her but the last one hurt.

I CAN'T BELIEVE YOU. HOW COULD YOU NOT TURN UP TO THIS?! GRACE WAS BRILLIANT BUT SHE'S IN ABSOLUTE BITS. YOU BASTARD.

I felt awful obviously, but it was 3am, I couldn't call and didn't know what to say in a text. I didn't get back to sleep, I was so guilty, guilty of being an absolute prick, that was for sure. My head was pounding too. I phoned at 7am hoping she'd even pick up.

"Hello?" After the first ring.

"Hi Grace, it's dad."

"Yeah, I know, it's a mobile phone."

"Look honey, I'm so so so sorry about last night, you have no idea just how sorry I am."

"Okay."

"It's not okay pumpkin, I'm an awful person. Can I come and get you today and do whatever you like?"

"No it's okay thanks."

"Come on, let's go shopping. I'll let you loose on whatever you like."

"No it's okay. I just want to stay here today."

"Shall I pop over and take you for lunch?"

"NO! I don't really want to see you today Dad. I can't believe you didn't turn up last night. All I could do was look at that empty seat at the front. Where were you? It was so embarrassing having that empty seat. I had to tell people you were ill."

"Tell me how to make this right? I just fell asleep."

"Fell asleep? Well thanks for thinking this wasn't important enough for you to stay awake for!"

"It's not that, I didn't mean to. Let me make this up to you please."

"This is just the tip of the iceberg though isn't it? You haven't been bothered about me for months. I don't need your constant attention but maybe every so often would be nice."

I had no answer, she was right.

"I can change that, I promise. I'm going to close on Tuesdays as well."

"Don't bother, you'll probably just need it to sleep."

"I won't, let's make it our day, every week."

But the phone was dead. Two minutes later she text to tell me not to try and make it up to her, especially today. Then Lucy called just to make sure I knew what an arsehole I was and not to try and get hold of Grace for the rest of the day. I sat down and felt really shit. My head was still hurting and my gut was wrenching.

The rest of the week I'd text Grace without reply. I was told by Lucy not to head over because I wouldn't be allowed in. I knew I'd been an absolute dick in all this but Stuart asked if it was a bit extreme. It sounded like it but like Grace said, it was just the final straw. It wasn't too far away from Grace's seventeenth birthday and I had to make it right for that. I finally got a text towards the end of the week but it basically said that she'll come over and work on Saturday but only if Chad was working. He was and she came over but pretty much just to make the point that she still wasn't talking to me. Teenagers with shitty dads, I get it. I wished this headache would go though. I couldn't think straight and had no idea how to make this right with Grace.

I needed to take more time away from the van but it wasn't that easy. The only person who could do the pies was Grace. I was pretty sure Stuart and Chad, stupid name, couldn't cope without me and Syd was also not really talking talk to me either. So she wouldn't help.

"Chadley Cooper!" I called him over. "Any chance you can see how I can get into your mate's good books?"

I called them mates as I was in denial but I think they were boyfriend and girlfriend now. But I didn't want to even think that was a thing.

"I don't want to get in the middle of it."

Fair enough but I wasn't accepting that. "Listen Chad, I just want to talk to her, she won't even entertain the idea. Surely you can ask her to meet you somewhere and I'll just be there instead?"

"No can do boss."

"How about I'm not your boss anymore then, how about I sack you if you don't do this."

He looked at me a little shocked.

"Scrap that, sorry mate, I didn't mean that. I just don't know what to do here."

"My best advice," started the lad who wasn't nineteen yet, "is to just leave her for now. I know it's not easy but she needs to get her annoyance out of her system. She's seventeen and seventeen year olds are complicated, especially girls."

"How many seventeen year old girls do you know then?!"

"Just the one and she's complicated."

Syd walked in and came and sat down.

"Alright?" I quietly said to her. "How's Grace doing?"

"Do you care?"

"Right, this is bollocks. I've moved here to be with her. Okay my eye has been taken off the ball recently but I am here for her."

"It's been about a year that you've not been taking her to do fun things or have quality time with her. She misses it and can't get through to you. This was just the straw that broke the camel's back."

"I see that, but how long is she going to punish me for?"

"Seventeen year olds ar...."

"Complicated?" I interrupted. "Yeah I keep hearing this. She's not even seventeen yet."

"It's not just that though Tom," Syd said as she came to the chair next to me. "A daughter needs a father to set the standards that she judges all men. When you don't spend time with her and brush her off, it's good that she's kicking off about it, she's not going to stand for any shit. But if the most important man in her life treats her with flippancy, eventually she'll think that's just what men do."

"I would never ignore her," Chad piped in.

"Shut it Chadley Wiggins. I bloody need Mr Perfect here don't I? I get it now and I just want to make it right."

"Just give her time, she'll have to process things herself. It might take a few days or a few weeks but it'll be okay eventually, I promise," Syd said, putting a reassuring hand on my knee. The door opened and Stuart walked in.

"Guess what?! I'm back on the market. Spread the word so I can spread my love!"

Stuart had actually settled down a bit in the last year or so, he had even got engaged. Not only engaged but engaged to a Muslim and she was from a strict family of Muslims. This was the first I was hearing about the great romance dying.

"Really? I thought I was working on my best man speech?"

"I was never getting married, let's get that right. I got engaged to get laid."

Stuart had been greatly accepted into this woman's family. Despite him not being Muslim (they let that go), there was definitely no nookie before nuptials.

"Tell us what happened then," Syd prompted.

"Chadley Walsh, go and find something to do, this is not for young ears," Stuart said with a wave of his thumb.

He sighed but thought better than to moan, and he left. "I'll see if Grace wants to meet up," he said, smirking at me. Little shit. But I'd have done the same.

"Well, you know I was telling you she was desperate to shag, but she couldn't, apparently, but she could still get herself off whenever she felt like it. Well my plan was to be there when she was right randy."

Stuart had to spend most time with her at her family home as she couldn't stay at ours but he told us her dad was good. He had a living room that the parents and little brothers would sit in and a room next door with a T.V in for Stuart and her so they could have at least a little privacy.

"Anyway, I decided to stick a little bit of porn on."

"In the room next to her whole family right?" Syd asked.

"Yeah," Stuart answered, as if it wasn't a crazy idea. "Anyway, we're watching it and sort of touching and kissing and she's saying all sorts of dirty things. So I'm thinking this is it, I've cracked it, we'll pop up to the bathroom and have a quickie."

"How romantic. I'm sure it's just how she pictured her first time," Syd rightly said.

"Well no, I reckon she probably pictured her first time with a big bearded bloke that smelt of camel or something," he replied.

"Why?" Syd and I both asked.

"Shut up, that doesn't matter. Anyway, she says to me that she's going upstairs so I say, okay, I'll follow you up in two-minutes. She then tells me, 'No, I have to do this on my own until we're married.' So I'm like, 'Fucking hell. Can I at least come and watch?' This was a no too and off she went. So I'm sat there, hard as a bloody iron bar, wondering how she's upstairs strumming one out and I was sat here with a hard on about a foot away from her family. So I was like, fuck this, and took myself off to the downstairs bog to empty my load."

"You really are a vile human being you know that right?" Syd stated rather than asked.

"That's not the worst bit though," he said.

"Oh god," was all I could muster.

"So I've crept off past the family and I'm in the loo tugging away and I'm thinking this will be out in no time but as it's about to come out I hear one of her brothers walk near the door so it sort of goes back in almost, but I'm not leaving it there, it hurts. So the boy must go because I can't hear him and I carry on, but it's not a quick one now, so when I finally do get there, the old boy is getting red raw but I had to get it out of me. As it is coming out the toilet door opens and her mum is standing there. It shot out as I turned in shock and went all up her dress."

Both Syd and I had our head in our hands.

"So I tried apologising but by this point her screams had brought the whole family seeing what had happened and I still hadn't put this, well pathetic, withdrawn penis away yet. I was thrown out and told never to come back. So that was that. Back on the market."

"That is gross."

"Yeah well, what you gonna do? She's been forbidden from ever seeing me again so it's not worth even trying."

"He best not put the word about where you work," I said.

"Don't worry, I told him I worked in an office, not dishing out pulled pork pies here."

"I think I've been put off pulled pork for life now," Syd said.

"You haven't ever pulled a man's pork before anyway," Stuart responded.

"You say that like it's a bad thing squirty," Syd soon quipped back.

"It'll be interesting to see just how much this bit of jiz actually hit this woman as you tell the story more. I bet it just dribbled onto the floor by your feet really," I added.

"Probably, but next time I tell it, it'll be hitting her in the face."

That story made me feel even more unwell than I already was. I still couldn't shift this sodding headache and now I actually felt sick.

Grace turned seventeen a couple of weeks later but still hadn't really taken me back into her regular days like I'd have hoped. We were talking and texting but it was one word replies from her most of the time. I tried gifts, no good. I took a whole week off to spend each day with her but she just got fed up with me so I was back in work after three days of that week. I asked if she fancied the island but that was a definite no-no.

I saw her most days though, but that was it, saw her. She was normally my way, just seeing Chad.

It was our dance at her seventeenth that finally won her back round. I'd been taking dance lessons for the last three months so it surprised her when I suddenly knew how to move.

Not that there's many moves to do to Louis Armstrong but she got my thinking. She was also looking as beautiful as ever. And she was smarter than ever. During our dance towards the end she told me all was forgiven. It was like somebody had lifted a bad spell on me. I felt so relieved.

I held her tightly and as the dance ended I said to her, "I really wish you could see yourself through my eyes. You're everything I'd ever hoped for plus a lot more princess."

"I think I'm a little old to be your princess anymore dad!"

"You'll never be too old. You'll always be my princess." I kissed her on the forehead and waved Chad over.

"He's a nice fella this one," I said, and winked at her.

"I know," she replied with a reddened face.

As Chad walked past I grabbed his arm gently and told him never to hurt her or I would make a pie flavour out of him. It was just something I thought needed saying, although I knew him well and how much he liked, probably loved, my daughter. Young love.

Over the next year everything was great. Grace was at a catering school in Singapore but only had to be there three days a week so the rest of the time she was with me. Well, us, me and Chad, okay, Chad. Stupid name. But it meant I saw her a lot. I was there for the good times and the two, only two, occasions that they'd had a row. But I was the one she came to each time she needed or wanted advice. Take that Lucy!

The trouble I was having was how busy we still were and how my headaches were getting worse. I felt like I needed to go on about a three month cruise. These headaches, stress and exhaustion I put them down to, had been off and on probably for over a year. I thought I'd arrange an appointment and book a holiday. I was pretty sure that's all I needed. A break and maybe some pills. But where should I go on holiday? And could I get Grace to come? I doubted it as we'd probably have to bring Chad too.

As it turned out, once I told Grace about my holiday plan she actually said that she could look after work for me. I was planning on going at Easter, so still about four months away at that point, Grace would be eighteen and I could spend this time getting her up to scratch. I had no doubt she could do it, she had done it. But I'd always been there.

Plans were set. We had a good and exciting few months coming up. Starting with Grace's birthday next week.

TWENTY FOUR

It was a spectacular bash. At Singapore's finest hotel. She deserved it. I paid for it despite Lucy's protests. The pie shop was clearing over RM2,000,000 a year, so that was around four hundred-thousand English pounds. I was minted! Not through lack of hard work mind.

The Bates' had come over as had Paul and Debbie. CK couldn't make it but it was good to see the others. There were over five hundred guests and all had come to see Grace and how she had turned into the perfect young adult. She hated being centre of attention but she was glowing. She had best not be pregnant!

We did our dance towards the end of the evening and finished to a huge round of applause. It was a shame there weren't more guests is all I could think, I felt like showing her off to the world. She was so happy. And she had no idea what was about to come.

Not from me, but Chad had approached me, and Syd actually, to ask for her hand in marriage. Grace's, not Syd's, just to clarify. I told him to fuck right off. It was my instinct I suppose. But as he got up to walk away I told him to sit down and we all talked it through.

He was a gentleman, considering he was Australian, that wasn't bad. He was hard working, I knew that first hand. He had a rich dad, and most importantly, he was besotted with my Grace. *My* Grace, if I accepted this would I still be able to call her that? Syd was popping open the champagne before I really processed it but they were right. She was young and that worried me but as Syd said, they'd been together and in love for years.

He proposed the night of her birthday. She gleefully accepted and I saw right there and then that, despite their young age, they'd be just wonderful together. Raising children and growing old together. Plus, I reckon I could pass on my business to them and retire at fifty. Only six years to go!

Grace grabbed me after the proposal and told me that she loved me and she knew this was a strange moment in a dad's life but this was everything she'd dreamed of.

"Okay beautiful lady. Just don't be pregnant and watching daytime T.V and letting all your years of hard work go down the pan!"

"Ha, no chance of that dad. If anything, I'll work and he can be the mum!"

"Or just don't get pregnant yet?!"

"Durrr, I know dad, people have babies in their thirties all the time now. I think we can wait a while."

"Good. I don't want to be a grandad at forty-four. Anyway, you okay from next week? You're in for full pie training!"

"Wild horses wouldn't keep me away!"

And with that I let her get back to her party and I went and ordered the largest scotch I could.

I was extremely happy for her and Chad, and how great she was turning out. Apparently the wedding was getting planned for the following summer. I couldn't wait for it. The bill, I wasn't too keen on, but the day I would make sure would be the happiest day of her life.

But after my results from the doctors I wasn't even sure I'd be there for it. I ordered another large scotch.

TWENTY FIVE

I had my holiday booked for the end of January, I couldn't wait for Easter. That meant I had a whole six weeks to get Grace up to scratch, and Chad to be fair, he was going to be a part of this after all but I mainly wanted to spend the time with Grace. So I made sure we were in there from 12-4pm and then Chad came in with Stuart at 4pm ready for opening. Grace had her own place now with Chad, it was here Danga Bay. It was here because it was my apartment. I'd moved into a house, still in Danga Bay but on a housing section so as an engagement and eighteenth present I'd given them my apartment. I say given, I was paying the rent, it wasn't mine to give. I'd bought this house though. Things had been good financially. So they were living there, and Stuart had got his own place a while back so it wasn't a case of them getting their own place with a sex-craved, weird lodger.

The next six weeks were six of the happiest of my life. If it was a movie, this would be a montage with something like *Golden Years* by David Bowie playing over it. Or as it was a movie, probably *My Girl*. We laughed all the time, we had food fights, singing, dancing, putting the world to rights all whilst I was showing her how EXACTLY to make the pies. I hadn't budged in all this time on the quality and still intended that to continue. I knew Grace would, she was naturally a gifted cook and had the serious attention to detail that was required. At least to start with, it would become second nature before too long. I was like a robot, but not in these six weeks. I felt rejuvenated. All thanks to Grace.

We spoke so much about what she intended to do with her life, and despite the fact she was only a couple of months away from qualifying as a full blown chef, she was adamant she wanted this life.

"It's such a success dad. I'm so proud of you and I want to expand," she said one day as we sat down for a break.

"Expand? What, stick an extension on the end of this motor home?"

"Don't be silly! I mean in another part of the world, well, Asia somewhere. People can't get enough of them."

"That sounds great. Hard work though. I still haven't got around to doing the dessert van next door, it's just got seats and tables over there for people coming here."

"Exactly! We need more space, more staff, more ambition, more, more, everything!"

"Blimey. Calm down. World domination will have to wait. It's a case of walking before you can run."

"But you've been walking now for a couple of years, slow coach. I know you're nearing fifty but come on!"

"Cheeky sod. I'm not even forty-five yet!"

"I'm only teasing. But come on, imagine it. *Pie's from the Skye's.* You will always have this one but Chad and I could look to start another one at some point in the next year, Singapore, KL, Thailand, Bali. Wherever. The world will be our Oyster. Or Pie."

"*Pie's from the Skye's* hey? I like it. Trouble is beautiful, you're not going to be a Skye soon."

"I'm not taking his name!"

"Really? Does he know this?"

"Oh yeah, it was a deal breaker."

I thought this was great.

"And you don't just like *Pie Guy* then?"

"Dad. I don't know if you've ever noticed, but I'm not a guy."

"That you are not Princess. I like your thinking though. Maybe over the coming months we'd add a sub-name under *Pie Guy* and get it to say *Pie guy: Pie's from the Skye's*. Then eventually we'll lose the *Pie Guy* bit". It was more of a statement - we were doing it - than a question.

"That would be utterly brilliant dad, and don't ever worry about us not pulling our weight. I see how much you've put into this, there's no way I'd ever give less than 100%. Chad as well."

I believed her. She had always had the same attitude and I was so pleased she wanted to take this on.

I still didn't know how to tell her that I was ill. I didn't want to tell her but is that fair?

It was the start of December when I got called back to the doctors after he ran some tests. The pills just weren't working and I'd even eased back at work. But my headaches were getting worse and were moving all over my head. After the results came back as inconclusive, he sent me for scans. Best thing about healthcare here was the speed of it, you had to pay for the privilege and I'd always been an advocate for the NHS kind of guy, but in this instance I wanted a quick answer. But after the scan, maybe I didn't.

It's one of those age-old questions. Would you rather know when you're going to die, or for it to just happen? I could always see both sides. One, you can do anything you'd always wanted to do, in theory, if you knew, but it's bloody depressing. Whereas the other option means you don't even have to think about it.

I was back in my doctor's office when he told me the news. Straight forward with no beating around the bush that I had a tumour on my brain. And that it was the size of a grapefruit apparently. I wondered how? How can that fit in there without there being a lump sticking out of my head. It was my first thought and probably not the right thing to be thinking about.

"Okay," I was obviously stunned. "What's the plan from here? An op? Chemo, radiation therapy?"

"Well Tom, I'm afraid not. There's nothing we can do. I'm sorry."

"What? Nothing at all?"

"I'm really sorry but it's been caught too late. Chemo would maybe give you a couple of weeks longer but the pain and suffering that brings in itself doesn't outweigh the reasons for not having it. But obviously, that's your decision. We can organise it straight away."

I couldn't believe my ears. When I think back to it, it feels like an outer-body experience, I'm looking down on both of us as he is delivering the news.

"Okay, right. What we looking at then doc, months? Years?" Big gulp. "Weeks"?

"Hard to say for sure but you're looking at six months, a year tops."

"I'm forty-four!"

"I'm really sorry Tom. Can I put you in touch with our therapist?"

"Forty-four." It's all I could muster. I must have said it five or six times.

I left the office in a daze. What else could I do? I spoke to the therapist and got a second opinion but not a different outcome. I decided against prolonging anything as I didn't think I'd have the strength to go through chemo, especially for the sake of potentially a few days.

I'd also decided not to tell anybody. I couldn't. I should but I couldn't even begin to imagine Grace in such a position as having to be told this. Especially as it was the biggest year of her life coming up. It was a shame I was going to ruin it. I was told by the therapist not to hide it and by one of the doctors that it would be impossible to hide. But I was going to try.

I'd try and put it out of my mind and enjoy this next few months. Starting with spending as much time with Grace as possible. I kept my holiday date but I didn't go to Thailand like I had originally planned, I found, in Singapore, a retreat where they'd try different medicine on cases like mine. I never really believed in any of that but I thought that now, where's the harm in trying?!

August 14th was the date set for Grace's wedding. We were in January when I made myself a promise that I'd be there to walk her down the aisle. Fuck whatever was growing in my head.

After the six weeks with Grace and having the best six weeks of my life (off the back of receiving the worst news of my life), I knew she was going to be even better than me. She had the knack but also a bit of flare and business nous, in fact, she was ten times better than me. Long after I'd gone, I could imagine a hundred of our places all around the world. I was so confident in her and proud. And Chad, stupid name maybe, was also a genuine, good, bright guy.

I got back from my retreat, expensive and ultimately, useless. I relaxed a lot but no changes in my misfortune. One of the worst things about it was waking up in the morning, obviously waking up was a bonus as that wasn't a given anymore, but every time I woke up I felt fine, for about a second before remembering.

I'd kept it all to myself for months. I hadn't told a soul. I was losing weight and generally looked pretty shit but I think I was covering myself well. *Yeah, can't eat, I've got a stomach bug* or *I've had the shits for about two weeks,* were my tried and tested answers if anyone ever asked. Not that many people did, bit weird to ask, *why do you look so shit then?* It reminded me of when I was younger (I was spending a lot of time thinking about the past, parents, friends, old pets, everything and this came into my head and made me laugh). When I was about twenty I had to catch a bus, I'd like to say my car was in the garage but I think I was a full on bus wanker, and next to me at the bus stop was a rather large lady. I had been there a few minutes and made eye contact and asked her, *'When's it due?'* and she just glared at me before saying, *'Alright you skinny prick, I'm overweight but I don't need idiots like you taking the piss, I'm not fucking pregnant alright?!'* I remember just looking back at her in shock, she must have been having a bad morning. *'I meant the bus, when's the bus due?'*

It was late June when I got found out. I collapsed at work and the next thing I knew I woke up in hospital with Grace asleep in the chair next to the bed. It was time to come clean.

I told Grace what was going on and it was worse than the day I found out. She was just shaking her head and saying no repeatedly, she was in shock and denial I suppose. I told a little white lie and said I only found out the week before. I don't know if she bought it but she certainly wasn't going to question me.

"We'll get the best doctors in the world here," she said.

"It won't make a difference princess."

"Well we can fucking try!"

It was the first time I think I'd ever heard her swear. I got her to sit down on my bed and pulled her in for a hug.

"We can't, there's nothing that can be done, best thing we can do is just concentrate on your wedding and make sure you're presentable on the day hey?"

"No way am I getting married now. We'll postpone it until next year when you are better, that's non-negotiable."

"Sweetie."

"No."

"Listen to me."

"No, I won't. You're fighting this! WE'RE FIGHTING THIS!"

"We can't. It's not a fight that can be won."

"There will be something. I'm going start researching now."

"Grace?"

She was wiping away the tears that were just flooding down her face.

"It's okay. It's okay. It's a shit hand but I'm okay. My job in life was obviously to make sure you have become what you have become. I've done my job. I wouldn't change a single thing about you."

"I can't dad, I can't take this in. I won't take this in."

"Chad is going to be there for you from now on. And don't worry about this," I said, pointing at the tubes coming out of me. "I'll be right as rain for your wedding day."

"Oh my god dad. No. This isn't fair!"

"No, what wouldn't be fair is if this was you. I've done what I needed to do."

"But..."

"Shhhh," I pulled her in for a long hug. "One thing that does disturb me though is Chad's name."

"What about it?"

"Well. It's fucking awful isn't it?"

She gave a snotty exhale of a laugh all over my lovely hospital gown. But stayed where she was and did for an hour which was lovely. Or would have been if I didn't really need to wee.

I spent the run up to the wedding here in the hospital. I wasn't well enough to leave apparently. Grace, Chad, Syd and Lucy were great and we did all the arranging and planning from in my room. It was a nice hospital to be fair, much nicer than the one that greeted Grace on her first day in this world, I was telling her. I could see even Lucy welling up at the story.

Stuart couldn't cope with seeing me. He just cried every time he came in but I needed to get him on board with the new regime. Made sure he knew Grace would be calling the shots. He expected that and I think he arranged to swap with Syd permanently so Syd would work with Grace and Chad and he'd do the bar. But I never knew if that was to be the case.

It was getting closer to the big day and I was getting better. I was actually getting worse medically really but I was definitely getting ready to get out of here. I knew I was going to die in this room so I'd cleared it with the doctors that I could have the day and night for the wedding as long as I paid for a medical orderly to be with me all day.

"Sure, I'll stick him on the list. Fish or lamb?"

TWENTY SIX

The day was here. I was up and ready to go. I couldn't get ready on my own, I could barely do anything and I looked eighty-four not forty-four, but I was ready. Dressed in my fancy suit I was picked up by Brad and we went to meet Grace at the hotel. The wedding was all taking place in a lovely hotel in Singapore, the wedding party would stay the night before and the night of the wedding. I could only do one so chose the night of. Then, Grace and her new Mr Grace where going with Brad to the airport and flying off to Fiji for two weeks. That had been arranged by Lucy but I had to promise Grace I'd still be about when she got back.

I got to the hotel and met Grace in her room. Everyone else had gone and we had ten minutes to ourselves. She looked absolutely stunning.

"You're simply breath-taking," was all I could manage.

I don't know if it was how I looked but Grace started crying. So I started crying.

"Come on, you're going to ruin your makeup!"

"Oh dad!"

I couldn't find anything else to say to her really. No pearls of wisdom or words of advice, just to enjoy the day. *Wow,* I thought. I had sorted my speech though so had to save enough energy to get through that. I felt pretty bad for Marvin, he was my nurse and had to come everywhere with me that day. I drew the line with Grace's room then and also when I walked her into the ceremony, that would have been well weird.

We got to the doors of where the ceremony was being held and I took a quick thirty second breather. We'd walked across the lobby getting snapped by our own paparazzi and some people that were just there. It was an effort. It was such a shame that I looked like a heroin starved pensioner and I suppose always will on Grace's wedding photos.

At the door Grace grabbed my arm tightly and said, "Let's do this dad. Thank you so much for being you."

"Don't be silly my little princess, sorry, not princess!"

"I'm only a princess because you've always been my king."

The music started and the doors opened and I walked her down to Chad. Stupid name.

The ceremony was great, bit long and I was tired. Marvin was doing very well with me. After the gasps had calmed down from Grace's entrance, her beauty shining like the sun, people took to their seats. I did my giving away bit and was grateful to take my seat. My biggest worry was collapsing and ruining the whole day.

The reception was good too. Very fancy. Marvin said it was the best lamb he'd ever had. Fuck you Marvin. No, Marvin was a good guy but hardly left my side, it was like having the Grim Reaper following me. Which I suppose he probably was really. I got through my speech but not the one I had written, which was longer and a damn sight funnier but I just didn't have the energy. The last ounce of energy drained out of me when I started my speech and everybody I knew in the party was weeping. I didn't want this to be the memory of the day. Grace was also struggling to fight back the tears so I basically just said how beautiful she is inside and out and what a nice fella Chad was despite his stupid name, and sat down. I passed Grace my actual speech and apologised.

Stuart came up to the top table and grabbed it off her and read it out. It was good even if I do say so myself. Bits about when she was sixteen, she said she wanted to be a gynaecologist and I didn't believe her until one day she decorated the hallway through the letterbox. Then all sorts of made-up jokes and many moments of happiness she'd brought to my life. And a couple of lesbian jokes obviously.

The day moved onto the evening and Grace was getting ready for her first dance with Chad. After that apparently I was up to dance with her. They tried telling me I didn't have to but I said there'd be no stopping me. Grace said she'd hold me up for all of it if needed.

As Grace and Chad took to the floor and started dancing there was a tap on my shoulder. It was Kate. I could have cried. More than I already had been.

"Hey you," she said, and gave me a big well-wanted hug.

She looked lovely. Gorgeous as ever and like she hadn't aged since I left. She'd got married and had a baby in that time and I was so pleased for her. I used to have lingering hopes that she'd follow me out here and to be fair it was nearly two years before she found her new man, Jack. But how it's turned out, I'm glad that it never happened.

We didn't have long to talk as I was about to get up and dance, or lean on Grace for a couple of minutes but I spoke to her quickly without letting go of her hands in front of me. I could see how upsetting it was for her to see me like this but I didn't want to let go. She was trying to say things but kept welling up and couldn't get her words out. I'd recently, on Grace's request, changed the deeds of my house over to Kate. Grace was right, it was more Kate's home than hers and she was more than happy to see it go to Kate. I'd obviously sorted my will so Grace got everything else, not that that is why Grace did it. She did it because it was the right thing to do. There was probably a Will & Grace joke here.

"Thank you," was the quiet word I picked out amongst whatever else she was trying to say.

The Bride and Groom dance was coming to a finish. Kate told me I'd have to come and meet Jack later, and Ethan, their one year old. I said I'd love to. The jammy bastard.

She leant in and kissed my cheek and gave me a hug and whispered in my ear;

"She looks absolutely breath-taking today, you should be very proud."

And with that she turned and walked back to her family. Her family. Oh what could have been. I had no regrets about coming here, how could I? But my one wish would have been Kate coming too. I didn't ask about Connor, I made a mental note to *not* ask about him later as well.

As I watched her leave, I was struggling to not watch her if I'm honest but I heard my name getting called up onto the dance floor. Oh god. DON'T COLLAPSE IDIOT! In fact DON'T DIE NOW was going through my head as Marvin helped me onto the dance floor and handed me to Grace. My Grace.

We took hold of each other, I was slightly leaning on Grace but also holding my own,and pretty well I thought. The start of We have All The Time In The World started, just that lovely musical intro. I could have melted. Grace told me we were dancing to Luthur Vandross which I quite liked but this was so bloody obvious now, I should have known!

As we started I couldn't form any words, they were stuck somewhere in my throat and would not come out. Grace knew and just held me tighter as we started to move our feet. Then, on the big wall behind the floor, all of a sudden videos started playing on it. Shit the bed. It was a video of me dancing to this with Grace on her first birthday. Who even filmed it?!

"Jesus, look," I said to Grace, turning her to see it too.

"I know dad."

"My god, look how young I look."

"Look how young *I* look!" Grace laughed, she had a point.

The video carried on playing and it was a combination merged into one from every single birthday dance we had ever had, through every single birthday of Grace's. I couldn't take my eyes off the screen, whilst still slightly moving our feet.

"How has this happened?" I asked Grace as a tear rolled down my face.

"Every year somebody had filmed it. Mum did the first one but we gathered them up from Stuart, Bates, Paul, Syd, even a couple of my old friends had some. I didn't know myself until about a month ago."

"It's incredible!"

"You'd best thank mum, she's the one who came up with this idea and got a whizz from her office to make it into this."

Great. I'm going to have to die liking her now.

The Louis Armstrong song only lasts about three minutes, which was always one thing I was grateful for as I didn't have to dance and embarrass Grace for too long, but because of the videos the song played again and we just carried on moving our feet and watching it. We got to the end of the second time round and we were on birthday eighteen so I knew it was coming to an end. I didn't want it to. When it did, I pulled my head a bit away from Grace and looked at her in her face. She was crying but had the biggest smile I'd ever seen.

Neither of us could speak. We didn't have to.

As Grace walked me off to the side, back to Marvin, who was living his best life (he had attacked the buffet *again*), I noticed absolutely everyone looking at us. I suppose they would be, and many of them in tears. I didn't want this today. Today was about Grace, and Chad, I didn't want him to take a back seat to bloody me. I lifted Grace's arm and waved Chad over and put their hands in each other's and gave them a shove onto the dance floor and everyone followed them on as the music went up in tempo, thank god. I sat down and watched everyone. Mainly Grace who was being picked up, emotionally and physically, by Chad. She looked so happy with him.

I didn't move for the next hour. I just watched everyone enjoying their evening. I had a few guests, most I didn't know to be honest, come over and tell me how wonderful Grace is and thanks for today but I was losing energy. I asked Marvin if we could go up to my room. He said okay and disappeared to grab my stuff, and probably a bit more food I guess. I turned in my seat to face the table and sat there. Talking away were Stuart, Paul, Debbie, both the Bates and even Kate was sat there too. How long they'd been there I wasn't sure, I'd been engrossed in the dance floor.

I just sat and listened and spoke when asked something. It was like going back in time. It was like most Saturday nights for many years. It was great. Marvin came back ready to get me out of my seat.

"Let's give it another hour hey Marv".

TWENTY SEVEN

When I did finally think it was time to go, I realised I'd actually stayed at that table for nearly two more hours. I didn't feel ill, I felt normal. I met Kate's husband Jack and their cracking little kid Ethan. Jack seemed a nice guy, Kate deserved that and I told her that too. I got up and said goodbye to all my friends and we got together for a big group hug. We made plans to meet up again the day after tomorrow at the hospital before they flew back. They asked for one big picture but I didn't want to be in it. I took a mental picture of all of them as I was helped away by Marvin.

We stopped when we saw Lucy. I called her sneaky little cow for sorting that video sequence. And she called me a pie-making moron. Fair play.

Syd came over and gave me a hug and said goodnight. "Breakfast at 10 tomorrow okay?" she said and I nodded.

"See you then. What time does Grace leave for Fiji again?"

"Think Brad is taking them at noon," Syd said as we turned and looked at Brad dancing like a daddy longlegs on ice. "If he's in a fit state of course."

"Okay, I'll say goodbye from here in the morning, I think *'not starvin' Marvin'* here has to get me back for twelve."

We said our goodnights and I headed towards Grace. "Night my favourite daughter," I said as I gave her a kiss and a hug.

"Night dad," she'd had a few I could tell. I didn't want her getting upset again now.

"I'll see you for breakfast yeah? And wave you off to Fiji."

"You will. Thanks for today dad. Thanks for everything," and she hugged me again.

"No problem. Now sod-off and get pissed."

"Yes sir! I'm only gone for ten days so have a think about what you want to do when I'm back. I'm sure Marvin can orchestrate an escape plan for a nice lunch somewhere."

"We'll sort it definitely," I replied as Chad came over. He just shook my hand and then hugged me. For well over a minute.

I was put into bed by Marvin and closed my eyes. I was knackered. And was feeling absolutely awful. I wasn't sure if I'd make that lunch with Grace, I decided I'd best make tomorrow a proper goodbye.

At 7am the next morning I was woken by a banging at the door. It was Chad and Syd asking if Marvin could come and help them, Lucy had fallen and banged her head, he told me to wait there and he'd be back in ten minutes. As he left I was thinking, *wait here? I'm not going off to spin class mate.* I did start to get up though. And the room was swaying. My cancer had spread through-out my body very quickly, I wasn't bothering with meds and all that annoyed me now was that I felt like I had a hangover without having a drink. Talk about rub it in.

As I looked up Stuart was in my room. He told me to hurry and got me dressed as quickly as he could, scooped me up and carried me out the room.

"What are you doing?" I said rather calmly as he carried me like a small child.

"It's a surprise. Ere, do you know who you remind me of now? Benjamin Button, BUT you know, erm, right near the start of the film."

"Brilliant. Thanks for that."

He took me downstairs and put me in the back of Brad's car.

"See you on the other side chief," he said as his voice broke and he choked back a cry as he looked at me for that fraction too long. He knew and I knew, we wouldn't ever see each other again. I tried my best not to think too much about it. I didn't have the energy.

But also, what the hell was going on now?!

"It's okay dad," it was Grace already on the back seat. "I'm stealing you."

"Erm, you're going to Fiji in a few hours!"

"I am going to Fiji, yes. But not until Christmas. We put our honeymoon back."

"What, why did nobody tell me?"

"Because you wouldn't accept what we are about to do. You wouldn't let me."

"Well that depends on what the hell it is?!"

"Just relax dad, trust me. It's a surprise."

"What about Marvin?"

"Don't worry about him, he's having *your* breakfast."

"I can't believe you're not going to bloody Fiji."

"It's fine dad. Fiji will still be there at Christmas."

"I know but I've paid for a bastard bottle of Champagne and strawberries to be there when you arrive!"

"That's really sweet of you dad, I won't be there to drink it but don't worry about it," she said grabbing my hand.

"Easy for you to say. It was four hundred quid."

We travelled without much to say really. Grace was struggling not to cry and I was struggling to stay awake. I did sleep a bit of the journey and when I woke I knew exactly where we were.

Brad pulled into the jetty.

"What have you done Grace?"

"Come on."

We said goodbye to Brad. He hugged me for over a minute, again. I guess people generally just didn't know what to say to me. Well, especially Brad.

We made it not only onto the boat, but across the water too. It was only a twenty minute journey I suppose.

The boat was just for us, as normal. We got to the island's jetty and I was helped up by two of the male staff members. They obviously knew that I needed help, Grace must have planned this for a while, the devious little sod. All the staff were the same staff as ever. They wheeled me down the jetty into the reception area and then to the restaurant side of it where we had some breakfast.

After breakfast we spent the day on the beach. I don't know why, I wasn't fussed about my tan but it felt good to feel the sun. Grace spent most of the day chatting about her plans with life in general. The business that was going to be world-wide apparently. Two kids, first one at the age of thirty. She had no plans of ever going back to England. Except maybe to open up *Pie's from the Skye's* shops, obviously. It was a great day. Just to be back here and being just with Grace. I was sure this would piss Chad off, I'd want to spend my first married day with my new wife. I raised this with Grace, she'd simply said that they have the rest of their lives to spend together and this idea actually started with Chad's suggestion.

As the sun started to drop, I felt like I needed to sleep. Grace asked if I was okay and I just told her I was tired.

"One last sit down on our jetty dad? Before bed?"

"Abso-bloody-lutely. Garcon, my chair."

Grace took me down to the far end of the jetty. I managed to get myself out of my chair and onto the seat on the jetty and Grace sat next to me and put a blanket around us both. One of the women came and put two mugs of hot chocolate on the table in front of us.

"Jumping in?!" I asked her. She smiled and said, "You first Mr Tom."

And I was tempted. If I didn't think my legs would snap trying to get to the edge.

We took a sip from our hot chocolates and sat quietly watching the sun dip and listened to the waves.

"I can't believe it's so long since we have been here," I said, breaking the quiet.

"I know, I miss it."

"That was my fault. I dropped the ball for a while when it came to you and I'm sorry Grace."

"Don't be silly. Our little misunderstanding we'll call it hey? That actually brought us even closer really didn't it?"

"It did. I suppose everything happens for a reason."

"Sometimes that reason doesn't seem fair."

We sat quietly again. Until Grace said, "Somebody told me the other day, when I was talking about you and wondering why life had been so cruel, that a good father will leave his imprint on his daughter for the rest of her life. I just wanted you to know that you certainly have."

The tears were being fought back again. But I don't think I had the energy left in me to even cry. "That's lovely to hear. Really lovely Grace. I'm just sorry I won't see you become the woman you will become."

"I know dad. It's just not fair." It was silent again except for the gentle ripple of water before Grace spoke again. "Hey, it's your birthday tomorrow. That's almost been missed hasn't it?"

I'd closed my eyes. "Yeah," I let out a little laugh. "I'd almost forgotten too."

"We'll plan what to do for it when we get back shall we?" she asked.

I'd fallen onto Grace's shoulder. As my last breath was escaping, I could hear the gentle waves as I listened to Grace speak through her tears, hearing her lovely voice. Picturing her lovely smile.

 My Grace.

"No rush though hey dad? We have all the time in the world."

The End

Printed by Amazon Italia Logistica S.r.l.
Torrazza Piemonte (TO), Italy